Also by Ellis Blackwood

"Among the finest historical cozy mysteries of our time" – *Cozy Crime Reads*

The Samuel Pepys Mysteries

Mr Pepys's Stolen Diaries (ellisblackwood.com)
Book 1: The Brampton Witch Murders
Book 2: The Plague Doctor Murders
Book 3: The Coffee House Murders
Book 4: The King's Court Murders
Book 5: The Frost Fair Murders
Book 6: The Drury Lane Murders
Book 7: The Brampton Ghost Murders
Book 8: The Crown Jewels Murders
Book 9: Jacob's Last Standish

The Quill & Page Victorian Mysteries

Book I: The Belgravia Phantom (summer 2026)
Book II: The Whitechapel Orphan (summer 2026)

The King's Court Murders

The Samuel Pepys Mysteries Book 4

Ellis Blackwood

Vintage Mystery Press

ISBN: 978-1-0687027-3-0

Cover design, editorial & historical fact-checking: Tim Brown, A.S.C. (Rtd).

Cover illustration licensed from shutterstock.com.

For Mary Neal, my historical mystery takeover competition winner, via the wonderful Cozy Mystery Lovers / Meg's Cozy Corner group on Facebook.

He tells me how the King hath lately paid about 30,000l to clear debts of my Lady Castle-mayne's; and that she and her husband are parted for ever, upon good terms, never to trouble one another more.

From the diary of Samuel Pepys

Scan for website and social media links

Contents

Chapter One

Pepys in a Pickle

Samuel Pepys, the esteemed naval administrator, paced behind his desk, muttering to himself. His newly shorn chestnut hair and snug periwig seemed to insulate not just his head but his troubled thoughts.

Seated before him were his young personal inquisitors, Abigail Harcourt and Jacob Standish, who was wondering whether to tell Pepys that he appeared to have trodden in something untoward.

"What perplexes you, sir?" asked Abby.

Pepys ceased pacing, placed his knuckles firmly on his desk, and leaned towards the inquisitors. His brown eyes bulged and his cheeks were flushed. "A parliamentary committee has been undertaking its yearly assessment of my naval accounts, Abigail, and I fear they will discover irregularities." As he huffed, his breath condensed in clouds before him, despite the presence of a glowing coal fire in the room. "It has plagued my dreams."

The date was Monday 1st October, 1666, and London was embracing a bone-deep chill after the previous month's devastating conflagration. Still, pockets of fire continued to burn about the city.

It had been a week since Abby and Jacob concluded their previous investigation, concerning murder among London's coffee houses. Pepys had granted them some free time in which to collect their thoughts and tend to much-neglected household duties, following their hectic baptism into the art of inquisition.

He had also found Abby lodgings in a small apartment within the same residential housing that Pepys and his wife, Elizabeth, inhabited, on Seething Lane, a healthy stone's throw from the Tower. It had cost him nothing, being supplied grace-and-favour by his own employer - the King's navy, for whom he acted as Clerk of the Acts - which pleased him mightily. Truth be told, it was a repurposed storage room.

Not that Pepys's former maidservant, aged nineteen, minded. It was the first home that Abby could call her own and she had spent the week transforming it to her taste, within her scant means. A keepsake here, a woollen blanket there. Unable to afford coal, she relied on scraps from the Pepys household.

Pepys had promoted her to the role of his inquisitor following the success of their second investigation, concerning the murderous Plague Doctor at Deptford docks. But that was little more than a fortnight ago, and he had not yet paid Abby her new, increased wage.

Jacob, for his part, had returned to his elegant townhouse on Strand Lane, where he rehired the servant he had sacked in a fit of delusion, believing he could maintain his own household. As he had quickly discovered, he could not.

The house was his late father's. Sir Miles Standish had been Surveyor to the Navy Board and a friend and colleague of Mr Pepys, who had agreed to look after the lad upon Sir Miles's deathbed request. Thrust into the role of inquisitor, Jacob was still learning the ropes.

A gangly sort with bushy eyebrows that met in the middle, what he lacked in confidence he more than made up for in enthusiasm and fortitude. He also possessed a keen eye for detail, and while Abby - self-educated with the help of her printer father and then the kindly Pepys, who had taken her under his wing - had proved to be the brains behind an operation, Jacob was at its heart.

These unlikely inquisitors made, they had discovered, a fine team.

"Why did you summon us here, sir?" Abby asked Pepys, twirling a strand of her fiery red hair around a finger. "Have you another investigation for us?"

Pepys regarded her with exasperation. "I do not, Abigail. I was not placed upon this Earth to provide for you victims of ungodly crimes. My mind is presently a whirlwind of navy business." He paused, still distracted. "If you wish to be of service to me, perhaps you might impress upon Mr Pett, the Master Shipwright, that I require the costings of timber from Scotland as a matter of some urgency? Hmm?"

Jacob furrowed his extravagant brow. "Sir, while I am not personally acquainted with Mr Pett, I…"

Pepys sighed. "'Twas a rhetorical question, Mr Standish."

"Then why summon us, sir?" Abby persisted.

Outside the leaded window, across Seething Lane, St Olave's bell chimed once. Eighty-seven of London's churches had been laid to waste by the recent fire, but not St Olave's, Pepys's church. It had survived by a whisker, saved by the wind driving the flames westward, away from its medieval walls. More pragmatic than pious, Pepys brooked no talk of miracles.

When the bell chimed a second time, he stood upright and blinked. "King Charles!" he exclaimed. "Indeed! That is why I did summon you, Abigail. I met with His Majesty yesterday and he informed me that he is eager for your company. It is high time we paid a visit to his court at Whitehall."

Under her breath, Abby groaned, and Jacob cast her a glance. She dared say nothing.

The kitchen maid, Mary Blythe, appeared in the doorway between the study and Pepys's chamber. "I bring fresh fruit," she announced, cradling a wooden tray of apples, pears and grapes.

When her master beckoned her forward, she placed them on his desk, glanced down and winked at Abby, her friend and former colleague. Receiving no response, she grimaced and retired from the room.

"What *is* the matter, Abigail?" Pepys asked. "Yourself and Jacob, my personal inquisitors," he puffed out his chest in its cotton shirt and silken waistcoat, taking credit for the wisdom of the appointment, "saved the King's life and he wishes to express his gratitude. What harm can there be?"

"None, sir," she replied, her turquoise eyes all out of fire.

Jacob raised a tentative hand. "Sir…?"

"You are no longer at school, Mr Standish!" Pepys snapped. "What is it?"

"I believe His Majesty has eyes for Abigail."

The older man - Pepys was 33; Jacob had recently turned 22 - laughed ironically. "It would be a curious state of affairs if he did not, Jacob! There is not a handsome young lady in the land who the King does not have eyes for…"

"But sir…" Jacob interjected.

"*And that is his regal prerogative.*"

Abby could contain herself no longer. "Master Pepys…"

"You may address me as Mr Pepys, Abigail, since you are now…"

"Mr Pepys, I am sure the King's attentions are wholesome…"

Both men snorted.

"Abigail, if you do not wish for the King's attention then simply tell him so. It served Frances Stuart well. Her games of the heart drove the poor man quite mad."

Abby clasped her hands together and eyed Pepys imploringly. "Sir, 'tis not only that. I'm not remotely suited to the grandeur of the royal court. I am but a servant girl…"

Pepys opened his mouth to cut in, but she continued, "His Majesty is surrounded by ladies in sumptuous gowns made by tailors from Europe, and by dukes and duchesses and knights and ambassadors. By rich gentlemen with more money than I would see in a thousand lifetimes. *The King's court doesn't befit me.*"

"Yet you acquitted yourself admirably there in your previous investigation."

"Aye, sir, in the heat of the moment." Her freckled cheeks had turned bright red.

Jacob popped a grape into his mouth. "Sir, if I may speak?" When Pepys nodded, he continued, "It seems to me that we have little choice but to accede to His Majesty's request. For he is king."

Pepys placed his hands flat on the desk. "Precisely, Mr Standish. I could not have put it better myself."

"But…" Abby began to retort, only to be silenced by Pepys slamming down a fist.

"You are no longer my servant, Abigail Harcourt!" His voice was raised, his temper unleashed. "You are a personal inquisitor, employed by Mr Samuel Pepys, adviser and confidante to Charles II himself, King of England, Scotland and Ireland. You would do well to remember that." Calming himself, he added with an arched eyebrow, "Or perhaps my appointment was made in error? Perhaps you are ill-suited to a position that warrants such honour?"

Abby shook her head firmly. "Nay, sir, I assure you. And I'm eternally grateful for all your kindness."

Pepys smiled. "Kindness, it may be, yet my faith in you is entirely warranted. I am no fool. You will acquit yourself at court most commendably. Of that I am certain." He glanced across at her fellow inquisitor. "'Tis Jacob who does concern me."

Jacob laughed, then stopped when he realised that Pepys was serious.

Amid the brittle silence, a clock ticked on the mantelpiece.

It was an expensive gilt-brass clock by the esteemed German horologist, Georg Christoph Lutzenberger, gifted to Pepys by a naval supplier currying favours, and one of which he was immensely proud. Several of his influential guests remarked upon the intricacy of its detailing, which was captured for a moment in a shaft of early-afternoon autumn sunlight.

The study walls were lined with custom-made bookshelves in oak, crafted by skilled navy carpenters - another perk of Pepys's job - bearing the weight of so many leather-bound tomes. He allowed Abby to read his books, and sometimes they read aloud together, knowing that she was quick-minded and keen to learn. Precious few masters would have done the same, and she was aware of it.

Pepys's sturdy oak desk was strewn with letters and ledgers, alongside a selection of feather quills, an ink stand and a sand-shaker, with which to dry the ink. A notebook lay open in front of him; when Abby peered to inspect the pages, she saw thinly scrawled shorthand text and thought to herself, *He's been writing his diary.*

Spotting her doing so, Pepys slammed the book shut and slipped it beneath a pile of ledgers with a self-conscious cough. When Abby caught his eye, he glanced away. *What's he been writing?* she wondered.

Once a plan was agreed – the three of them would travel by water to Whitehall Palace the following morning – the inquisitors rose to leave.

"Ah! Mr Standish!" Pepys cried.

Jacob hovered awkwardly, neither seated nor standing. "What is it, sir?"

"I omitted to ask after your sister. She attends to the King at his court, does she not? Be so kind as to remind me of her name."

Jacob slumped back down and Abby watched his expression, intrigued. As she was aware, Jacob's family was a sensitive subject.

"Her name is Anne," Jacob replied, and offered nothing more.

"Are you fond of her?" Pepys asked.

As Abby retook her seat, Jacob tugged on a periwig curl. "Indeed," he replied. "She is my sister."

"And her… position at court. Do you approve?"

"'Tis not for me to say, sir. 'Twas my father's wish. It made him proud."

Pepys chuckled. "I have heard she is quite a handful."

Jacob replied in barely a whisper. "Some say she is a law unto herself."

Sensing his discomfort, Abby spoke up. "What think you of the King's mistresses, Mr Pepys?" she asked.

Rather than taking offence, he guffawed, slapping the desk. "I have ever admired your bluntness, Abigail, and long may it endure. However." His mood shifted in an instant. "I must caution you - watch your tongue at court. The walls have ears and I trust none there. All vie for the King's favour and would stab their mother in the back for it. 'Tis a dangerous place, and men have lost their lives over a single ill-conceived word."

A persistent tapping noise became apparent. Following the direction of the sound, Pepys and Abby saw that it was Jacob's right foot, tapping manically. His head was bowed and his jaw clenched.

"Does something ail you, Mr Standish?" Pepys asked.

"Aye, sir," he replied, then met his employer's gaze. "What know you of my father's politics? 'Twas my impression that he was fiercely loyal to the King..."

"Indeed he was. A fine, upstanding gentleman and a firm friend. His loss remains greatly mourned."

Jacob interjected, "...Yet, during our previous investigation, I heard innuendo from more than one man, among them a Member of Parliament, that leads me to believe he may have been..." He hesitated.

Abby shot Jacob a sharp look, willing him to back off.

"May have been what?" Pepys asked.

"A republican spy, sir."

The room fell very still. The clock continued its metronomic ticking, and outside a hawker announced his wares. "Chestnuts! Sweet roasted chestnuts!"

"Mr Standish..." Pepys began sombrely.

Jacob leapt from his chair, suddenly animated. "We both believe he was murdered, sir! For what possible reason? My father was admired by all! If what I heard is true then…"

"Be seated, pray," Pepys spoke over him, motioning for calm. Then, exhaling, he added, "Sir Miles was indeed admired by all, to my knowledge, and I find the very thought that he was traitorous to the King abhorrent…"

Jacob nodded furiously.

Pepys raised a finger. "However, once again, I must counsel the utmost caution. Mention nought of this at court. 'Twould be the gravest of follies."

"But…"

"Promise me, Mr Standish." Pepys fixed his protégé's gaze. "Else our partnership will become impossible to maintain, which would sadden me greatly."

Jacob's long face fell and he glanced sideways at Abby, who nodded. "Then I humbly make that promise, sir," he said.

"Excellent!" said Pepys, rising to his feet and shooing the inquisitors away, as if they were errant children. "We meet tomorrow at eight, at Custom House Quay." Pausing, he sniffed the air and wrinkled his nose. "By the by… what *is* that foul odour?"

"I fear you have trodden in something untoward, sir," said Jacob, pointing at Pepys's leather shoe.

Chapter Two

Return of the Kilgore Brothers

Abby and Jacob made their way past the burnt-out ruins of Custom House, once a three-storey brick structure with octagonal towers, towards a cluster of Thames watermen waiting in their wherries. Numbered in their thousands, watermen ferried passengers up and down the congested river; they were the lifeblood of the city, and in constant flow.

"See who it is!" came the cry from a Montero-capped man standing in one of the wherries. "Oi, Osbert, it's old Wrong Shape!"

Osbert, seated beside him, glanced toward the approaching Jacob from under the brim of his hat, tutted, and returned to staring at his boots.

"Fie," Jacob muttered to Abby, "'Tis those impudent Kilgore brothers again."

They had been rowed to Deptford docks by Clement and Osbert Kilgore, Mr Pepys's favoured Thames watermen, on their way to investigate the Plague Doctor murders. Expert rowers, they had proved to be, however they had also delighted in riling Jacob in particular.

He had hoped it was their day off.

Having stayed overnight at Strand Lane, Jacob was dressed in one of his father's more ostentatious outfits – a rather snug-fitting, purple velvet doublet with gold embroidery, flouncy breeches and large-buckled shoes – which he felt might suit the royal court. The formality of his appearance was marred only by his trusty periwig, which looked like something coughed up by a cat, but from which he refused to be parted.

He had met up with Abby at her new lodgings at some ungodly hour, eager to please Mr Pepys with their punctuality. However, as they approached the appointed meeting place, they realised they were rather early.

She had shown him round her apartment, which did not take long. Despite being damp and cold, the single room with rope bed in one corner was spotlessly clean and tidy. It helped that Abby owned precious few possessions: a wooden chest, a kettle in the fireplace, a saucepan, a few utensils (all donated by Pepys), and a one-eyed rag doll on the bed, wearing an uncertain smile.

The space already smelled of Abby, Jacob noticed – an earthy sweetness that made him feel content.

A temporary wooden quay had been swiftly erected after the fire, restoring access to one of London's most popular river stops.

"Well then, Wrong Shape?" asked Clement, sucking on a clay pipe.

"My name is Jacob Standish," replied Jacob, looking down into the Kilgores' wherry. "*Mr* Standish, to you."

Whipping off his grubby cap with a flourish, Clement bowed. "Pray, forgive me my impertinence."

Wisely suspicious, Jacob nodded curtly.

"You see, sir," Kilgore went on, "I may 'ave mistaken you for a young gentleman I had in my wherry not two weeks past. Accompanied by a young lady, much like yours. Most beguiling, she was." He leered at Abby, who curled her lip. "And that young gentleman, well… 'e was the wrong shape."

Jacob clenched a fist. "I am of a mind to leap into that boat and…"

"I wouldn't advise that, sir."

"Why forever not?"

"You might fall in, like you did last time."

"I did not fall in! Did I, Abigail?" he spluttered, turning to Abby for support.

"Nay, Jacob," she replied, then after a pause added, "Only your hat did."

Clement Kilgore doubled over with laughter; even the usually morose Osbert's shoulders shook with mirth.

Abby stepped onto the wherry's gunwale, surveying the river beyond teeming with craft. While Clement rushed forward to help her into the unstable boat, his brother remained rooted to his seat, glowering at a hovering gull.

"Don't you worry about him, mistress," Clement said, gesturing toward Osbert. "Finest oarsman that side of this boat."

"You made that joke last time," Jacob pointed out witheringly.

"He makes that joke every time," muttered Osbert, roused from his introspection. "One day I'll drown meself in the river. Escape his ceaseless tedium."

Clement took Abby's hand and guided her to the seat at the stern. "May I say, mistress," he said, as she smoothed her petticoats before sitting, "how delightful you look?"

"You may not," she replied.

Besides her tatty old maid's clothing, Abby owned a single gown worthy of display, which had been given to her by Pepys. Since she was devoid of attire approaching royal-court standard, he had once again come to the rescue, albeit with the loan of one of his wife's elegant outfits. (Abby was petite, narrower than Elizabeth, which was remedied by the judicious use of hidden pins.)

She wore a lace-trimmed silk gown in deep green, with a fitted bodice and full skirts. The neckline, she was pleased to note, was particularly modest. She had tied up her hair and secured it in place with ribbons, leaving long, soft strands to frame her face. Covering the ensemble against the October chill - and a harsh wind bowling up the river - was a hooded cloak made of dark wool.

Mr Pepys had offered her a string of his wife's pearls, which she had politely but adamantly refused, petrified of losing such an expensive item.

Jacob plonked down heavily next to her, causing the boat to rock wildly and Clement to stagger to retain his balance.

"Careful!" the waterman yelped. "Don't want you goin' under! I know what's lurkin' down there."

Abby pulled the hood tighter around her head. "What is lurking down there, Mr Kilgore?"

Jacob dug her in the rib. "Do not indulge the oaf's nonsense."

"T'ain't nonsense, Wrong Shape. I've seen it with me own eyes, what goes into this river, and much of it ain't pretty. Had a dead whale in me river once. Might still be down there, far as I know. Lurkin'."

Jacob was about to protest when the Kilgore brothers sprang suddenly to attention and began bowing and scraping as if their lives depended upon it. "Mr Pepys, sir!" they sang in unison. "'Tis an honour to serve you!"

Mr Pepys had indeed arrived, carrying an artfully carved cane and wearing fine leather gloves. Allowing himself to be guided into the wherry with a waterman at each hand, he addressed Jacob. "I see you have a feather in your hat, Mr Standish."

Self-consciously, Jacob felt for the plume. "Aye, sir, I fancy it makes me appear more fashionable."

"Oh, it does sir," said Clement, with not a trace of sarcasm. "Did I not just say, Osbert, how elegant and fashionable the young gentleman appears?"

Osbert, straight-faced, nodded. "'Tis true, Mr Pepys, sure as fish is fish."

Settling onto his seat opposite the inquisitors, his back to the watermen, Pepys spoke loudly for all to hear. "Are the Kilgore brothers not the finest waterman on all the Thames? In another life, they would have been gentlemen."

Clement thumbed his nose at Jacob, unseen by Pepys, causing Abby to restrain her fellow inquisitor in his seat.

And so the journey to Whitehall began.

Chapter Three

Shooting the Bridge

The sun was low in the sky, pale yellow like uncooked corn, glimpsed occasionally through light-grey cloud cover. The Thames, as usual, teemed with traffic. To the left was Southwark and to the right, the city of London. The sounds of rebuilding - the hammering and sawing of wood, the chipping of stone - drifted across the water.

Ahead loomed London Bridge, its southern half weighed down by towering buildings, while those on the northern end were gone, perished in the fire. Its nineteen arches were darkened in shadow, resembling blackened teeth awaiting prey.

"Are we shooting the bridge, sir?" Jacob asked Pepys, one eyebrow raised.

"Indeed we are, Mr Standish," he replied, as the wherry advanced on choppy waters towards one of the central arches. "I have experienced the feat many times, and I would trust no guides more than Clement and Osbert."

In his former role as an apprentice Royal Navy purser, Jacob had also travelled the river many times. Whenever a waterman offered to shoot the bridge - navigating one of the long, dark arches where treacherous currents swirled unseen, and hazardous debris often lay lodged - like many others, he would insist on disembarking and walking around.

Only once, mildly inebriated, had he broken this golden rule. Then, his wherry had snagged on a hidden obstruction and capsized in a sudden surge of the river. Jacob, unable to swim, would surely have drowned had the tide not swept him, panicked and swallowing the rank water, into the side of a Thames lighter, where he was mercifully dragged aboard. What became of his waterman, he never learned.

"Excellent," he told Pepys through gritted teeth. "What an adventure."

Catching Jacob's gaze while toiling at his oar, Clement winked.

As their wherry approached London Bridge, the churning sound of the river between the arches became increasingly apparent. Froth appeared on the surface of the mud-brown water, and the boat began to rock stern to prow over the lolloping waves. Rising and falling. Rising and falling.

Jacob turned to Abby and saw that she was clasping her hands in prayer, lips moving rapidly, her eyes scrunched tight shut. Unable to afford river travel on her servant's wages, the young woman had never experienced the like before – her beloved Thames so angered.

The lavishly decorated Nonsuch House loomed above the wherry. Viewed from the river level, its four tall storeys might well have been forty, as the onion-domed towers stretched endlessly into the drab firmament.

Pepys tapped Jacob's knee with his cane. He seemed entirely untroubled, Jacob thought, by their impending doom. "Nonsuch House!" Pepys called over the noise of the rushing water. "Built in Holland, dismantled, shipped, and reassembled here. Most ingenious!"

Grabbing for his hat, which almost blew off, Jacob nodded dutifully. "Aye, sir. Most ingenious."

"Hold fast!" Clement cried.

Jacob clung tightly to his seat and a gunwale, while Abby clung to him, burying her head in his chest. Noting their apparent ease with one another, Pepys smiled to himself.

As the wherry's prow reached the bridge's wooden starlings, glistening with sodden seaweed, the river's roar ascended to fever pitch. Beneath the arch of the bridge itself, the sturdy little craft was buffeted one way and then the other, rocking frantically. Every crash echoed as the daylight became subsumed by shadows.

Compelled to witness the experience, Jacob cast a glance at the Kilgore brothers. Clement and Osbert worked their oars in perfect rhythm, countering the river's intricate currents, their faces taut with concentration. Before him, Mr Pepys appeared to be humming to himself.

Spray flew, spattering their faces, as the river rose and crashed into the stained stone walls.

The boat tilted wildly, lurching them all to one side, and Abby let out a squeal.

"Fear not, mistress!" Clement hollered, heaving on his oar.

With a sudden surge of the water beneath them, the wherry plunged through the arch, out of the gloom and into calmer water.

Gradually, Jacob felt Abby's grip relax.

"Are we through?" she asked, her voice muffled by Jacob's coat.

He tapped her on the shoulder. "Aye," he said. "You may come out now."

Chapter Four

To Court

Once again, the inquisitors were forced to endure the sight of the charred remains of the city, which they had witnessed but a week ago from the same vantage point. Precious little had changed. It would take many months, even years, before London was rebuilt, and with it the shaken spirits of its inhabitants.

Sensing their despondency, Pepys piped up. "I have met with the King concerning the rebuilding of the city. The finest minds of his kingdom are gathering, among them my good friend, Robert Hooke of the Royal Society, and Christopher Wren, whose skill as an architect is greatly admired. Their work begins soon, and I am assured it will be a triumph."

"Where have all the people gone?" Abby asked.

"I am told many thousands of Londoners now live in tents, at Lincoln's Inn Fields, Hatton Garden and Covent Garden piazza. A sorry sight, if ever there were one." Pepys's mood visibly dampened, he changed the subject.

"My dear wife's attire does suit you most perfectly, Abigail."

Abby blushed, bowing her head. "The mistress is too kind, loaning me such an expensive gown."

Pepys inspected his cravat. "I confess I have not told her," he mumbled, as they pushed past Somerset House.

Jacob's house lay up there, beside the old Renaissance palace, and not for the first time in his whirlwind career as an inquisitor, he wished he were safely ensconced within its familiar walls. Abby had made it clear that she would feel deeply uncomfortable in royal surroundings, and it occurred to him that he felt no different.

Having previously helped to save King Charles's life, he had been permitted to kiss His Majesty's hand - a rare honour - but for how long would the goodwill linger? Historically, England's monarchs had been notoriously fickle; many a right-hand man had lost their head at the bark of a majestical order.

"Sir, what is it like - the King's court?" he asked.

Swivelling his head, Pepys glanced warily at the Kilgore brothers, who seemed intent upon their rowing. "Your sister resides there, Mr Standish," he replied. "Has she not informed you?"

Jacob pursed his lips. "I have not seen her since she left for the court. We have both been... occupied."

"What can you tell us of the King's mistresses, Mr Pepys?" Abby asked.

The older man's brown eyes misted over, and a small smile played on his lips. He said nothing.

Abby and Jacob exchanged a glance. "Mr Pepys?" she persisted.

Shaking himself from his reverie, Pepys blustered, "A fine lady, Arabella Wyndham. Among the finest. If only her tastes were more modest." Clearing his throat, he added, "There are others, as one would expect – Mistress de Valois; the young Tanner woman, Molly, who is as handsome as Mistress Wyndham, if a tad coarser… And, naturally, Mr Standish, your sister, Anne."

"Are they all on good terms?" Abby asked, before Jacob could react.

Laughing ruefully, Pepys shot the Kilgores a furtive glance, and leaned in close to his inquisitors, ensuring his reply could not be overheard. "They loathe the sight of one another, Abigail. 'Tis a veritable nest of vipers."

As the wherry rounded the steep curve in the Thames at Durham House, it began the final leg of the journey towards Whitehall Palace. Abby and Jacob had only recently followed the self-same route, accompanied by the old coney-catcher, Jim Quigley. Neither dared breath a word of it to Pepys. The less their master knew of their illegal activities, the better.

They were heading, they realised, towards the Privy Stairs – the entry to the court that Quigley had expressly advised against using, since it was heavily guarded and frequented by visiting courtiers and invited dignitaries. Now, it struck them both, they numbered among the invitees.

What good will come of this? Jacob wondered.

The stairs were located at the end of the Privy Bridge, a pier on stout wooden legs lined with royal out-buildings.

Having tied off the wherry, Clement helped Pepys out. "A pleasure as always, sir," he said, as Pepys handed him a shilling coin. Flicking it deftly to Osbert - evidently the Kilgores' treasurer - Clement reached out a hand to guide Abby off the boat.

While she and Pepys ascended the steps, Jacob stood unsteadily in the wobbling craft, ready to disembark. Clement whispered into his ear, "You'll stand out like a sore thumb in there, Wrong Shape."

It was just the confidence boost he needed.

The trio gathered at the top of the sodden wooden steps, stained with rust at each of its iron fixings. Across the pier, an identical set of steps ran down to the river, where another wherry was being moored by a grizzly old man in a hat.

A young woman helped herself off the boat, wearing a low-cut burgundy gown and tight-fitting, matching bodice. Her loosely curled auburn hair was tied at the back with a ribbon and her blue eyes glinted with mischief. She looked to be Abby's age, perhaps even a little younger.

"Sammy, ain't it?" she asked Pepys, as she strode up the steps, hitching her petticoats to avoid them trailing in slime.

Jacob's chin almost hit the deck. *Sammy?* he thought. *How dare this brazen wench address Mr Pepys in such an insolent manner.* He assumed she would be given a sharp dressing down.

Instead, Pepys was in the process of melting. "M…mistress Tanner!" he stammered, bowing. "How delightful 'tis to make your acquaintance once again!"

She held out a grubby hand laden with bejewelled rings, and he kissed it theatrically.

Mistress Tanner turned to Abby. The women were similarly petite. "Greetings, sweetheart," she said, casting her an appraising look and smiling broadly. "You may call me Molly."

Finally, she looked up at Jacob, towering over her, and wrinkled her nose. "What are you doing up there, eh?" Breaking into raucous laughter, she poked him playfully in the midriff and sauntered off down the pier towards the palace.

The inquisitors were left dumbfounded. "That was…?" Abby said.

"Molly Tanner, aye," Pepys cut in, then lowered his voice. "His Majesty's latest mistress. He discovered her at the theatre. She is," hiding his mouth behind his hand, he said under his breath, "*an actor*."

Jacob gasped. "But, sir…"

"Hush, Mr Standish," Pepys interjected, patting his arm. "Certain young women are making a name for themselves in these enlightened times, treading the boards."

Abby, who had never visited a theatre - seeing a play, even among the cheap seats, would have cost her a week's wages - was open-mouthed. Never before had she encountered a young woman who carried herself with such confidence, and who exuded such an irreverent attitude.

"Mr Pepys!" The husky, booming voice echoed through the archway beneath the buildings on the pier.

Pepys stood to attention. At the palace end of the pier was a vast barrel of a man in a fur-lined purple cloak, wearing an extravagantly coiffed grey periwig, flanked by two guards holding pikes. "Sir William Hakewill," he told the inquisitors. "The King's chief adviser."

"Come!" called Hakewill, beckoning impatiently. "His Majesty is expecting you."

Pepys began the introductions. "Sir William, these are my personal inquisitors, Mr Jacob Standish and Mistress Abigail…"

"I am well aware, Pepys!" Hakewill cut in sharply. "This young lady saved His Majesty's life, for which we must duly praise the Lord."

Jacob noticed one of the guards eyeing him suspiciously. The burly young fellow's face was familiar… *'Tis the one rendered unconscious by Quigley!* Jacob realised with horror. *When we stole into the Palace of Westminster under cover of darkness.*

Will he recognise me? Hastily, Jacob pulled his hat brim down over his eyes and lowered his head.

"Are we to meet with His Majesty, Sir William?" Pepys asked.

Hakewill gave a wry snort. "I said that the King was expecting you, Pepys, not that he is present. His Majesty has…" he paused, his voice laced with disdain, "more pressing matters to attend to."

"Might those same matters have arrived lately by wherry, on this very bridge?" Pepys asked.

Hakewill cleared his throat. He had a persistent, reedy wheeze.

Chancing a peek at the guard, who was still staring at him, Jacob lowered his gaze once again, his heart pounding.

"Sir William," said the guard, causing Jacob to start. "This gentleman…"

"Be silent!" Hakewill barked. "Mistress Harcourt, His Majesty has provided for you an apartment, which I trust will meet with your approval. I will show you there now. The gentlemen may accompany you."

Abby shot Pepys a horrified glance. "Sir William, I was not aware that I'd remain here. I thought…"

Hakewill bowed to her, a wry smile on his plump grey lips. "Nonsense, my lady. You are the King's honoured guest." Extending an arm, he ushered the party into Whitehall Palace.

Jacob, head resolutely downcast to avoid being recognised by the guard, had no idea in which direction Hakewill was pointing. Swivelling, panicked, he lost his bearings, took three paces forward and toppled off the pier.

Chapter Five

Little Anne

Constructed in the late 1500s, Greenwich Court Manor was an imposing brick-and-timber house built by Lord Nicholas Thorpe, Elizabeth I's Comptroller of Naval Forces. When accusations of embezzlement surfaced, Elizabeth allowed Thorpe to keep his head but took away his pride and joy: the house.

She gifted the estate to Sir Edward Standish, captain of the galleon Resolute, in recognition of his bravery alongside Sir Francis Drake during the defeat of the Spanish Armada of 1588. Standish, never one to avoid blowing his own trumpet, renamed the place Standish Hall, thus establishing the family's ancestral seat.

Above the studded oak main door, Sir Edward secured the family coat of arms: a lion, shield and griffon, with crossed-swords and anchor, beneath a rising Phoenix. It bore the Latin motto, 'Ex Umbra in Veritatem'.

One summer afternoon in 1653, Anne Standish had stood in the courtyard outside the grand house, gazing up at the coat of arms. Her elder brother, James, had teased her, saying the motto translated to "Anne Standish is a fopdoodle".

She was only six years old, and it had made her cry.

Their father, Sir Miles, had come running outside, disturbed by the commotion, and after giving James a sound thrashing – which Anne felt was only just – he had gently reassured her that the motto meant, "From the shadows into truth."

A year later, at the grand old age of seven, Anne recalled the event and wondered which she preferred, shadows or truth. She could hide in shadows from her siblings, then jump out and scare them. Shadows were exciting, she decided. But truth – her parents and governess had long impressed upon her its importance – felt like a heavy burden.

Turning, she surveyed the garden. The flower beds surrounding the lawn were a cacophony of colour, and the scrolled stone fountain her father had installed was sending limp jets of water into a wide, circular pond covered in lily pads. Having briefly debated hunting for newts in its green depths, Anne found herself lifting the latch on the heavy old main door and letting herself inside the big house.

Ahead, at the far end of the hallway, a wooden staircase led up and to the right, accessing the first-floor chambers. A suit of armour guarded the foot of the stairs; the Standish children had christened the silent sentinel Sir Egbert.

The walls were wood-panelled and recently polished by a servant - Anne could smell the beeswax. Flames flickered on thick candles set on wrought-iron sconces along the walls, and the flagstones beneath her bare feet felt cool, worn smooth by so many footsteps.

Either side were doorways. Hearing her siblings' voices through the first one to her right, leading to the parlour, she peered inside.

The ornate stone fireplace was cold, as sunlight flooded the space with summer warmth through three large leaded windows. The walls were oak-panelled, hung with decorative Persian rugs and European 'Wild Man' tapestries. Elsewhere, bookshelves and cabinets lined the walls, and a tall, wrought-iron candlestick stood in each corner.

The room felt cosy.

James and Robert, twins aged eleven, were engrossed in a card game, seated at a table in front of one of the windows. Their expressions of intense concentration - those extravagant eyebrows - were identical. Born mere minutes apart, under the twitching eye of the family physician, Phineas Quirke, they insisted upon dressing identically and wearing their loose auburn curls shoulder-length.

Visitors routinely failed to tell them apart, but Anne could: to her, they smelled different. Both shared that same musty boy-scent, but James, the elder, had a sweeter, more insistent note.

Elizabeth, the oldest of the Standish children, aged 14, was sitting perfectly upright on an upholstered settee. In her hands were an embroidery hoop and a needle threaded with silk. She wore a simple linen apron over a dusty-rose bodice, and a white coif topped her loose blonde curls.

"Come inside," she told Anne, on hearing the door creak open. "Don't hover there like a ghost."

The boys did not even look up, but her other sister, Margaret, did.

Elizabeth was the sensible one - the eldest - who took it upon herself to tell her siblings off and to order them around when the adults were absent. Margaret, 13, tended to ignore her, which could drive Elizabeth to distraction.

Margaret was curled on the wooden floor, making a daisy chain. "Who invited you?" she asked Anne.

"I invited myself," the little girl shot back, causing Margaret to smirk - it was what she would have said.

Anne stepped into the room, closing the door behind her. What game can I play? *she wondered.*

James and Robert had a pegging board, so she reasoned they were playing cribbage, which confused her. All that counting.

Anyway, they would not let her join in. They never did. The twins were inseparable and insular.

Elizabeth would shoo her away, she knew, like her mother did. Elizabeth was allowed to call their mother "Mama"; the others were obliged to use "Lady Standish" or "my lady". Anne knew her mother's real name, which she had overheard her father use on occasions. It was Honoria.

Honoria Standish put the fear of God into Anne.

"Can I help you make daisy chains?" she asked her bigger sister.

Margaret merely stuck out her tongue and swept her pile of white-and-gold flowers closer.

The children had seen precious little of their father of late, since war with the Dutch broke out. Sir Miles, the Navy Board's Assistant Surveyor, had attempted to explain the politics to his children one suppertime: "the English Navigation Act" and something about "fighting over trade routes". It all meant precious little to Anne, though she had noticed the twins becoming heated. Even Jacob, just two years older than her, had affected a form of indignation.

Where is Jacob? *she wondered.*

Although the boys and the girls were tutored separately by Mistress Winthrop - Constance, as she allowed them to call her, when her parents were absent - it was common knowledge that Jacob was having trouble with his studies.

Only the previous week, at the supper table, Lady Standish had been discussing the servants' wages with Sir Miles. The cook, Alice, had asked for a raise of her current £2 and 12 shillings per annum.

Lady Standish's waspish expression had alighted upon her youngest son. "Jacob!" she said sharply. "How much does cook earn per week if we pay her £2 12 shillings each year?"

Jacob, happily chewing on a gravy-smeared pork rib, looked up as if she had asked him to bring the pig back to life. While the twins eagerly nudged one another, Elizabeth's expression willed her brother to succeed, and Margaret just smirked.

Anne, seated next to Jacob, rested her small hand on his knee. It caused him to start.

"Um," he stammered, replacing the half-eaten rib on his plate. "If cook earns £2 12 shillings each year, and there are…" He paused. "Twenty shillings in each pound?"

While James and Robert could barely contain their glee, Lady Standish nodded curtly.

"If there are twenty shillings in each pound…" Jacob went on, counting out imaginary coins on his gravy-stained fingers, "then…" Having run out of fingers, he faltered and gazed pleadingly at his father.

Sir Miles, raising an eyebrow, only shook his head.

Anne was used to being treated like an unwanted toy by her siblings. She tended to counter that by acting up.

Striding through the parlour, she made for the mantlepiece above the fireplace. Displayed there were a matching pair of pewter cherubs; small, framed portraits of Sir Miles and Lady Honoria; a brass candlestick with five arms; and a porcelain teapot decorated with delicately painted birds.

The children knew they were not allowed to touch.

Anne turned around. Only Elizabeth was paying her any attention, glaring sternly.

Aware she was too short to reach the mantlepiece - having tried before - Anne grabbed one of the three wooden stools in front of the bookshelf and dragged it to the hearth.

"If you touch anything, I shall tell Constance," Elizabeth warned her sharply.

"But I want to play tea parties," Anne replied, mounting the stool and reaching for the porcelain pot.

As she turned on the stool, clutching the precious item in both hands, she swayed alarmingly from side to side.

Elizabeth did not move, but tightened, still glaring. "Put. That. Back."

By now, Anne had the full attention of everyone in the room.

Margaret was sitting cross-legged in the centre of the room, eyeing her youngest sister with amusement. Robert nudged James and the boys began clapping, accompanied by a chant, "Drop it! Drop it! Drop it!"

Teetering on the stool, Anne stepped to the floor. It was a long step on such small legs, and as her feet connected with the boards she stumbled forward, horror etched on her face, eyes fixated on the pot.

"Huzzah!" the twins cheered in unison.

Everything happened in a blurred moment.

Margaret smirked, Elizabeth sprang to her feet, the boys clapped, and Jacob entered the room to see his sister precariously cradling his father's precious teapot – a gift from the French ambassador, crafted from the finest Chinese porcelain. A rare and expensive gift.

In a buoyant mood, having finished his extra mathematics lesson, Jacob sprinted towards his youngest sister just as Margaret pushed out a leg. Blinded by his focus on the teapot, he tripped, sprawling forward, flailing for balance. Desperate to avoid colliding with Anne, which would send her into the stone fireplace, he twisted to one side. But his momentum was too great; as he fell, one hand swiped the pot, knocking it from her grasp.

It shattered on the hard floor.

Sliding across the polished boards, Jacob came to a halt at the hearth.

He turned and sat up, gazing in disbelief at the scene.

The room was filled with an ominous silence, the kind that stopped time itself.

Elizabeth, Margaret, James, Robert and Anne all stared at him, mouths agog.

"It… it… it was not my fault," he stammered.

The aftermath was as dire as the Standish children had feared. Yet Jacob took all the blame out of loyalty to his younger sister, whom he felt compelled to protect.

It was he who had taken the teapot from the mantelpiece, he insisted to his parents, and he who had stumbled carelessly, allowing it to slip from his grasp.

Standing all alone before the assembled family, Jacob was made to apologise to Sir Miles, then caned. As was typical for any family misdemeanour – for which the unruly Anne was most often to blame – he was made to run Navy Board errands on Sir Miles's behalf for one month. Additionally, given the severity of the crime, he was banished to sleep with the servants in the stables loft.

If Anne expressed her undying gratitude to Jacob's crestfallen face, his utter devotion only encouraged her to tease him further. On one occasion, she broke a chair leg while playing on it and quietly swapped it with Jacob's. When he sat down for dinner, the chair toppled backward. As he flailed for balance, his hand caught the edge of the tablecloth, sending plates, dishes and cutlery sliding and crashing to the floor.

He saw the guilt in Anne's eye, yet Jacob could not bring himself to cast blame on her. Sir Miles had drilled into him the importance of unerring loyalty, and Anne could only look upon her brother with amused admiration.

Chapter Six

The Apartment

While Jacob was fished out of the Thames by servants, Abby followed Hakewill and Pepys into Whitehall Palace. Although she was nervous, she could not quell a frisson of excitement. Only weeks ago, she had been a lowly maidservant. Now, at the King's own invitation, she walked the corridors of England's highest power. It seemed unreal, like a fevered dream.

"His Majesty's lodgings to your left," Hakewill explained, "Her Majesty the Queen's, to your right."

"Is the Queen in residence?" Pepys asked.

Hakewill coughed lightly. "These days, Her Majesty prefers the solitude of Somerset House."

In truth, both Pepys and Abby knew, she was tired of her husband's infidelity and the duplicitousness of his mistresses. The ungodly circus.

Pepys, wisely, left that unsaid. "And the Duke?" he asked, referring to Charles's brother, the Duke of York.

"In France, Mr Pepys, at the invitation of King Louis."

"Then His Majesty has the palace to himself?"

"Indeed he does," Hakewill replied with a sigh. "Indeed he does."

"He cannot...?"

"Hear us? Nay, sir. Doubtless, he is otherwise engaged with our recent arrival."

Past the royal apartments, the flagstone corridor narrowed, emerging into daylight at a wide, open walkway lined with timbered buildings. Smoke drifted overhead from the palace's countless fireplaces. Hakewill led them to the left, past an ornamental garden set behind the King's quarters, towards an oak door.

On the other side was a courtyard, where they were confronted by a three-storey building with a tall, gabled roof, grander than anything Abby had seen in the city. Its timbers were expertly finished and painted, its windows leaded in intricate diamond patterns, and the clay-tiled roof looked freshly laid.

"Your apartment, Mistress Harcourt," Hakewill announced.

It was all Abby could do not to gasp.

"'Twas, till recently, the Duke of Montford's lodgings. He requires them no longer," Hakewill added, leaving the Duke's fate to her imagination.

The interior of the house was still grander.

A brass chandelier, glowing with the flames of a dozen candles, hung from the high, beamed ceiling. The walls were lined with dark, polished wood panels, hung with rich tapestries, and an imposing stone fireplace, already ablaze, dominated one side. A heavy oak table sat in the centre of the room, flanked by gilt-edged, upholstered chairs.

The smells of smoke and polish lingered in the air.

"Oh my!" Abby blurted, immediately wishing she had maintained her composure.

Footsteps descended the staircase in the far corner, partially hidden by a heavy tapestry. A young woman appeared, roughly Abby's age, flush-faced, adjusting her coif as she bustled into the room.

Presenting herself before Hakewill, she smoothed down her apron. "I beg your pardon, sir," she said breathlessly. "I was tending the mistress's chamber fire and did not hear you arrive." Looking towards Pepys then Abby, she bowed.

"Your maid, Mistress Harcourt," said the King's adviser. "Do you wish her to be punished?"

The maid's dark eyes widened momentarily as she looked towards Abby.

"Good heavens, nay," Abby rather blurted out. "Indeed, sir, I must confess I would not be comfortable…"

Beside her, Pepys loudly cleared his throat.

Abby took the hint - she had a role to play, one to which the former maid herself was not yet accustomed. "That is to say, I would be grateful for the assistance. What is your name, girl?"

"My name's Betsy, mistress," she replied, wringing her soot-blackened hands. Her dark brown hair hung in long strands behind prominent ears.

"Would you wish for a footman as well?" Hakewill asked.

Abby smiled beatifically. "That won't be necessary, Sir William, I assure you."

After Betsy had been dismissed, returning to her duties upstairs, the two men took seats at the oak table.

Pepys looked expectantly towards Abby. "Will you join us?" he asked, nodding surreptitiously towards the seat beside him.

"Indeed!" she said, grinning awkwardly, pulling up the heavy chair.

"What news of His Majesty?" Pepys asked Hakewill.

The King's adviser exhaled deeply and pulled off his periwig, revealing short, matted silver-grey hair. "His life is an excess of pleasure, Pepys."

The men's easy familiarity suggested to Abby that they had shared similar exchanges in the past. Of course, she realised, as one of the King's confidantes and overseer of the Royal Navy accounts, Pepys would naturally have the ear of key courtiers. Still, she was surprised by Hakewill's indiscretion.

The King's adviser went on, "Only last week, I chanced upon His Majesty…" Hearing footsteps on the flagstones outside, he fell abruptly silent.

A knock came on the door and a servant entered, carrying a large silver tray laden with dishes. He placed it on the table, revealing a dinner that made Abby's eyes pop: plates piled with roast pheasant and venison, bowls of buttered carrots, parsnips and fresh greens, along with freshly baked bread and a carafe of wine. The aroma of warm yeast drifted up from the loaf.

Just as the servant was leaving, Jacob arrived, and the two became briefly wedged in the doorway.

Wearing a woollen cloak over a long nightshirt, clutching his own sodden clothing in his hands, he apologised profusely. "I became disoriented, I fear," he explained. "Lost in the moment's haste."

While Betsy arranged his wet clothing on an iron rack in front of the fire, Jacob took a seat at the table between Pepys and Abby. If he had been nervous before, he was now ashen-faced.

Abby shot him a resigned smile, but he just shook his head.

Although Pepys took it upon himself to explain his inquisitor's clumsiness – "And this is hardly the first incident!" – Hakewill seemed entirely unconcerned.

Stuffing pheasant into his mouth, the old adviser waved the blathering aside. "Mr Pepys, there is a far more important matter of which I must make you aware…" He stopped short, eyeing first Abby then Jacob. "Your inquisitors, sir - I am assured of their discretion?"

When Pepys nodded solemnly, Hakewill began his tale.

The previous week, he said, he had entered Sophie de Valois's lodgings unannounced, to find the King there with a number of other mistresses; among them, Arabella Wyndham, Molly Tanner and Anne Standish.

On hearing his sister's name, Jacob sat bolt upright. A gentle tamping motion of Pepys's hand quelled any exclamation.

"They were gambling, sir, as is their wont. What can I do, being but Lord High Treasurer!" Hakewill laughed ironically. "Before them lay a pile of gold coins, worth, by my estimate, two thousand pounds. *Two thousand pounds*, Mr Pepys! Sufficient to purchase a fine townhouse in Covent Garden - won or lost on the turn of a card!"

"What the navy could do with such a sum, Sir William."

"Indeed, sir. I am at my wit's end. I cannot control these women, for they have the King's ear."

"And more besides," Pepys added drily.

Abby stole a glance at Jacob. They could not believe they were privy to such inflammatory royal gossip.

"They are veritable agents of sin, Mr Pepys!" Hakewill declared, suddenly animated, pointing a quivering swollen finger at Abby. "And now you bring another into the royal palace!"

Pepys froze mid-chew. "I can assure you, Sir William," he blustered, quickly swallowing, "that Mistress Harcourt has no designs upon the King."

Vigorously, Abby shook her head in agreement.

"She is here as His Majesty's guest," Pepys continued, "having saved his very life mere days ago, and for no other reason."

Taking a gulp of claret, Hakewill stared at Pepys. "Very well," he said, setting down the goblet and turning his beady eye on Abigail. "The last thing this kingdom needs is another shameless, money-grabbing harlot 'neath the King's roof."

Reaching into his satchel, he handed Jacob a piece of paper. "A warrant of entry to the palace," he told him. "It allows you to come and go as you please."

Jacob glanced at Abby and allowed himself a satisfied grin.

Chapter Seven

Gone Exploring

When Pepys left with Hakewill on official business, Abby called Betsy down and offered her a seat at the table. The gaunt servant scanned the substantial dinner leftovers like a dog eyes a marrow bone.

"Help yourself," Abby told her.

Betsy flinched, as if scalded. "Nay, mistress, I dare not. 'Twould see me flogged."

Abby placed her hand on top of hers, and the young woman stared at it. "I'll tell nobody," she reassured her. "Neither will Jacob."

Jacob was busy taking second helpings. "I beg your pardon?"

"You won't… Oh, it matters not. Please, Betsy, help yourself."

The young servant needed no second bidding. With a quick check through the window that no one was approaching, she began shovelling food directly from the serving dishes into her mouth.

Jacob curled his lip.

"I too was a maidservant," Abby said quietly.

Still eating, Betsy regarded her with disbelief. "Nay, mistress," she replied between mouthfuls. "You are too elegant and handsome for that."

Abby felt her freckled cheeks grow warm. "I served Mr Pepys - the gentleman who escorted us here - for two years ere he made me his personal inquisitor. I..." She hesitated, aware it might sound boastful. "I know something of your burdens."

Slowly, deliberately, Betsy replaced the slice of venison she had just scooped from its plate. A look of distaste flickered across her features as she turned to face Abby. "You know nought of my burdens," she replied, a hint of a snarl in her voice. Then, catching herself, she added with more measure, "You women are all alike - prying and grasping. Go, plunder His Majesty's coffers. 'Tis all you're fit for."

As she strode towards the stairs, Abby leapt from her seat. "I'm not...," Abby began, only to feel Jacob's hand on her shoulder.

"Leave it be," he said.

The meal continued in awkward silence.

When he had eaten his fill, Jacob, hoping to lift Abby's spirits, cried, "Let us explore! How often do we find ourselves in Whitehall Palace?" Then, recalling their previous illicit escapades, he added, "At the King's behest, at least."

Abby, downcast, drew in her lower lip.

Outside, a bell tolled the third hour.

"I am eager to find my sister," he persisted. "You must accompany me and make her acquaintance. I feel certain you will become firm friends."

She looked up at him. "I'm intrigued to meet her, Jacob. You seem afeared to explain her."

He blinked a couple of times. "'Tis best you meet her yourself. She will tell the story with more gusto than I." Buoyed, he rounded the table, took her hand, and pulled her towards the door. "Shall we go?"

She resisted. "Jacob?"

He let her hand drop. "Aye? What is it?"

"You're wearing a night-shirt."

With Jacob changed into his almost-dry attire – albeit his leather shoes were still sodden – they left their lodgings. "Which way?" Abby asked.

"I have no idea," he replied, and they laughed.

The sky had bruised, and a fierce wind whipped around the little courtyard, sending autumn leaves swirling. From over the rooftops came distant sounds of footsteps and chatter, and the muffled clinking of so many servants and tradesmen at work.

"We should ask someone," said Abby, making for the nearest door.

Across the courtyard stood a tall red-brick building, which turned out to be the lodging house for Queen Catherine of Braganza's Maids of Honour. With the Queen currently in residence at Somerset House, only a skeleton staff remained, but a matronly woman answered the door and directed Abby to Anne Standish's apartments.

"What did she say?" Jacob asked, when Abby returned to him.

"We're to head for Banqueting House, taking the route back to the Privy Stairs, then veering left."

He nodded blankly.

"Come," she said, hoping not to betray her own fragile confidence.

Whitehall Palace, Abby knew, was a maze of old buildings - a rabbit warren of mismatched architectural styles. She had read up on the place in Pepys's library, as soon as her visit became inevitable. Forewarned was forearmed, she knew.

As they retraced their route, she related some of her learning.

The palace had begun life, she explained, in the 13th century. Then known as York Place, it was the residence of the Archbishops of York and expanded greatly during

Cardinal Wolsey's tenure. When, in 1530, Henry VIII's Palace of Westminster burned to the ground, he ousted Wolsey, seized the buildings, and renamed them White-hall Palace.

He ordered several sporting additions, including a bowling green, cock-fighting arena, real tennis court and the Tilt Yard, for jousting tournaments.

Henry married Anne Boleyn and Jane Seymour in Whitehall Palace and died there in 1547.

Subsequent monarchs, including their own King Charles II, had committed to further expansion. "'Tis said the palace presently comprises some 1,500 rooms," Abby concluded.

Jacob whistled. "Then we are likely to become lost."

When they reached the corridor leading to the King's and Queen's apartments, the inquisitors paused.

"Which way?" Jacob asked.

Abby gestured to the passage ahead, which veered to the left, where a pair of guards in royal livery could be seen approaching.

Both inquisitors halted and stiffened, bracing to be challenged, yet no such challenge came. The guards spared them barely a glance as they strode past toward the Privy Stairs.

Abby and Jacob exchanged astonished looks. It seemed they had the run of the place.

The corridor narrowed, took a sharp turn, and ended at a T-junction.

"Left or right?" Jacob asked.

"I do wish 'twas you who'd spoken to the Queen's maid!" Abby shot back.

To the right lay another courtyard, clustered with ornate Tudor-style buildings. To the left, the street narrowed further still, disappearing into shadows.

"Where is Banqueting House from here?" Jacob asked.

Hands on hips, Abby tutted. "I've no idea."

"Shall we ask somebody?"

"Aye, Jacob. 'Tis your turn."

Ahead was a red-brick building set over two floors, with a steeply sloping gabled roof and jettied first floor.

Pressing his face against one of its tall windows and shielding his eyes from the daylight, Jacob peered inside. He could make out… an eye. Somebody the other side of the window was peering back at him. "Yoo-hoo!" came the cry, muffled through the glass.

Jacob lurched backwards and fell over. As he picked himself up, he could hear the woman inside the house giggling.

Moments later, a door was flung open, and Molly Tanner appeared. She rushed up to Abby and enveloped her in a hug, as though they were long-lost friends. "What did you say your name was, sweetheart?" she asked.

"I didn't," Abby replied, since Molly had not bothered to inquire. "I'm Abigail Harcourt." She gestured toward Jacob, who was brushing himself down. "And this is my colleague, Mr Jacob Standish."

"Oh dear!" Molly exclaimed. "You can dispense with all that 'Mr' business with me, sweetheart. Ain't no standing on ceremony with Molly Tanner!"

Jacob straightened his hat. "And you are… an actor?"

Molly put a hand to her lips, feigning coyness. "You're too kind, sir. 'Tis my misfortune to be recognised throughout London for my work upon the stage."

"Forgive me, mistress," Jacob replied, "but I had no idea who you are. 'Twas Mr Pepys who informed me of your profession."

Molly's hand dropped, her expression darkened, and her voice lost all its cheer. "Oh. I see. Can't you afford to visit the theatre, sweetheart?"

Abby knew of Molly Tanner through Pepys. Born into poverty, she had scraped a living selling fruit in the pit of London's theatres, where her vivacity and alluring looks had caught the attention of an impresario. He had transferred her talents to the stage, where her rise had been swift.

She had drawn the King's eye only the previous year while treading the boards at the Theatre Royal on Drury Lane. By all accounts, His Majesty was smitten.

To avoid a scene, Abby cut in quickly, "We're looking for Jacob's sister, Anne Standish."

Molly's professional facade returned as she clutched her cheeks in mock surprise, her mouth agape. She clasped Jacob's wrists. "You're Anne's brother! How delightful! Anne is such a sweetheart. I adore her with all my heart."

According to Pepys, the mistresses loathed one another, but Abby let it pass. "Then you can tell us where she lives?"

"Why, we're neighbours!" Molly squealed, pointing toward the house next door.

Jacob was about to knock on Anne's door, his fellow inquisitor lingering behind, when Molly linked her arm through Abby's and drew her to one side. "Nay, you must accompany me, Abigail Harcourt," she said.

"But I wish to meet Jacob's sister," Abby protested.

"All in good time, sweetheart! All in good time. Charlie's staging a pall-mall tournament…"

"Charlie?"

"You know – His Majesty!"

Jacob had to steady himself with a hand on Anne's door.

"He's hosting a pall-mall tournament in the park, and all the mistresses will be there. And Loxley - you must meet him! He's a vision. Say you'll come!" Molly clasped her hands in a pleading gesture.

Abby glanced at Jacob, who gave a nod. Secretly, he much preferred to face Anne alone; he could not predict how his sister would react to his unexpected arrival.

Chapter Eight

Pall-Mall

While Abby had no wish to be associated with King Charles's mistresses, her inquisitor's instinct - or perhaps plain curiosity - compelled her to attend the pall-mall tournament. She had never played the game herself, though Pepys had often regaled her with tales of purposefully losing to His Majesty.

Charles would no doubt be present, and though the prospect mortified her, it seemed wise to face him sooner rather than later.

It was some comfort to have Molly for company - a friend, of sorts. At least the young actress hailed from a world not unlike her own, where families living by their wits fought desperately to escape the relentless grip of poverty.

Molly led her past Anne Standish's lodgings, out of the maze of streets and alleyways, and into a wide courtyard from which the rear of Banqueting House was visible.

So that's where it is, Abby thought, mentally sketching a crude map for future reference.

"Do we walk?" she asked.

Molly blew a raspberry. "Walk? To St James's Park?" she said, as if Abby had suggested they fly like birds. "Nobody at court walks. We'll take a sedan, sweetheart."

Despite herself, Abby felt a growing warmth toward the excitable young woman. Guided by her inquisitor's instincts, she ventured a probing question. "What can you tell me of the King's other mistresses?"

"Beware them all!" Molly laughed. "But most of all, beware Arabella. She rules the roost and has the King wrapped about her little finger. She'll have your head if you give her the chance."

"And the others?"

"Sophie de Valois spies for the French."

The statement was so blunt that Abby nearly choked. "And no one pays it any mind?"

"Hakewill allows it, for her wits are no brighter than a candle's flame. She was once betrothed to Loxley, but Charlie stole her away."

"Was Loxley not enraged?"

"Passionately so! Yet it was not long before Charlie grew weary of Sophie - once his eyes met mine."

Abby shook her head in disbelief. "Such a tangled web."

But Molly was far from finished; she seemed to revel in her tale. "'Tis said your friend's sister dallied with Loxley for a time, purely to vex Sophie."

"Anne Standish?" Abby said sharply. "What if His Majesty were to discover it?"

"Keep your voice down," Molly hissed. "The same whispers say he did - even threatened to take her head - yet she escaped his wrath. She plays a perilous game."

"And these whispers are true?"

"Who can say what's true? Trust is scarce at court, while deception flows more freely than wine."

"What of you? Can I trust you?"

Skipping ahead, Molly turned back to face Abby. "London adores me, and I delight all of London. 'Merry Moll,' they call me. I am but eighteen - so much younger than the others, and far more fun."

You didn't answer my question, Abby thought.

The two young women passed through an expansive garden surrounded by broad wooden walkways, with a central pulpit. Following the rear of Banqueting House, they emerged via Court Gate into the wide street Abby was familiar with from her previous investigation. Molly named it as Whitehall. There, to Abby's left, was the twin-towered Holbein Gate. Guards were stationed around the walls, as before, but the musicians who had played there on her last visit were gone.

Abby noticed a rank of half a dozen sedan chairs against the opposite wall, their liveried chairmen gathered in a group, smoking pipes and chattering.

"Ho!" Molly called across to them.

All dozen chairmen appeared keen to accept Mistress Tanner's fare, since a fierce debate broke out among them. At length, two pairs picked up their chairs by their long poles and trotted across.

"I've never ridden by sedan," Abby told Molly.

"You'll become accustomed to it," came the reply.

Abby had always imagined travel by sedan chair to be the height of luxury. And indeed it was - if hardly as comfortable as she had imagined. While her velvet seat was cushioned, the chairmen's rhythmic stride caused her to bounce lightly up and down, which soon became irritating.

The sedan chair itself was essentially a person-sized box, little more, despite its decorative touches. Tall and narrow, with glass windows - a royal prerogative, no doubt - it boasted heavy drapes, which she could have pulled together to travel incognito.

But Abby wanted to see. Since she did not intend for her courtly sojourn to last long, it was important for her to savour every possible experience.

She became aware of the pungent smell of stabled horses even before she saw them, as the chairmen carried her through a stone gateway, plunging her into gloom. Having passed the stable block, she emerged into a bright expanse of green. Abby realised she was in St James's Park.

Gazing out, she saw she was traveling along a tree-lined walkway. Between the trunks, manicured lawns stretched out, dotted with formal flower beds and clipped topiary. The wind had died down, and as the dark clouds lifted, people had come out to stroll.

In the distance, Abby glimpsed a long stretch of water where flocks of birds had settled. *The ornamental canal I read of*, she thought, recalling that it had been commissioned by Charles under the influence of French designers.

And then… She blinked, shook her head, and rubbed her eyes. When she looked again, it was still there: a beige-coloured creature, the like of which she could never have imagined, with a long neck and the hunch-backed body of a great horse.

It was nibbling leaves from one of the trees - a truly wondrous sight.

She called out to the chairmen. "What is that creature?"

"'Tis known as a camel, mistress," one replied, his voice quivering with each step. "From His Majesty's menagerie."

"Unholy, if you ask me," added the other.

The sedan chair was set down with a light bump, and Abby was released from her upholstered cage. Next time, she decided, she would insist upon walking.

Molly was already out of hers and flirting with her chairmen. On noticing Abby's arrival, she cut the discourse dead and took the inquisitor's arm. "Come," she said, making for a nearby row of tall topiary.

Between the rectangular hedges, Abby could see ladies in rich, sweeping gowns gathered chattering, each one holding a long wooden mallet.

The game of pall-mall, she thought, swallowing drily. *'Tis time.*

"Please, stay with me," she told Molly.

Striding purposefully, Molly merely giggled.

Ahead was a group of four people, courtiers given their expensive attire: three ladies and one gentleman. Abby was relieved to note that it was not the King.

Molly whispered in Abby's ear, "Sophie de Valois, Arabella Wyndham, Isabel March and James Cavendish, Duke of Loxley. Could you not just eat him? Incidentally, pay no mind to Isabel; her husband was lately accused of treason, so her days at court are numbered."

As the gathered courtiers spied their approach, Molly called out, "Yoo-hoo!" and quickened her pace, pulling Abby with her.

Abby suddenly felt small and out of place. In her mind, her borrowed finery from Elizabeth Pepys dissolved into the threadbare rags of her former life as a maidservant.

"What have we here?" It was Loxley, arching an eyebrow. In his mid-30s, he wore a billowing white shirt beneath a long satin waistcoat in emerald green, with a matching plumed hat. His lustrous periwig, Abby noted, was twice the length of Jacob's, and considerably better maintained. A scar ran down his stubbled left cheek, from cheekbone to chin. "Do you admire my scar?" he asked, his tone tinged with ribaldry.

Struck dumb, Abby could only nod.

"I received it in battle," he said, "defending the King's honour against ten war-hardened infantrymen."

Molly, still clutching Abby's arm, nudged her. "He received it from a gentleman who didn't take kindly to discover Loxley laying with his wife!"

The ladies laughed uproariously, and as Abby watched the duke's reaction, a small, furry white face emerged over his shoulder. It had a squat pink nose and two intent, coal-black eyes. As she gasped, the creature stuck out its tongue at her, and she recoiled.

The courtiers' hilarity only grew, while the inquisitor shrank, wishing she could vanish entirely. Molly, she noticed, was laughing as well, and Abby pulled her arm away in frustration.

"Do not be afraid of him," Loxley told Abby, his voice still laced with mirth. "He would not harm a fly. Would you, Figaro?"

The monkey began inspecting the duke's ear, pulling at the flesh with its tiny black hands and peering into the crevices.

"What is… Figaro?" Abby asked.

"Why, 'tis a capuchin monkey, my lady. Have you not seen one before?"

Indeed I haven't! she thought. *Unless such creatures live in Mr Pepys's filthy fireplaces.* She shook her head.

"You must excuse me, but…" It was the dark-haired woman on the left of the group, Sophie de Valois. She spoke with a similar accent to Pepys's wife, who was of French Huguenot descent. "*Who are you?*" It was more accusation than query.

"Is her face not familiar to you?" asked the woman next to her, identified by Molly as Arabella Wyndham; Abby knew her name from society gossip. "She saved Charlie's hide at that dreadful prize ceremony," Arabella continued. "What was the blackguard's name?"

"Guy Colborne," replied Loxley. "And we all know what happened to him!" he added, drawing a finger across his throat, to the group's general amusement.

"In truth, it was Kelburne," said Abby.

The courtiers recoiled as one. Even the monkey sat bolt upright and stared at her.

"What did she say?" asked the third mistress, Isabel March.

They all shook their heads.

"I said, his name was Guy Kelburne. Not Colborne."

"Oooh, we have a feisty one!" Loxley quipped, jauntily swinging his mallet.

"This is Abigail Harcourt," Molly interjected, before Abby could reply. "Of late, she was Mr Samuel Pepys's maidservant..." She paused, savouring the audience's disdain. "But now she is his...?" Molly looked to Abby for help.

"Personal inquisitor," Abby replied, as gamely as she could muster.

The King's mistresses feigned puzzled looks.

Arabella peered at her, as one might appraise a thieving mudlark. Her raven-black hair was piled loosely on her head, tied at the back with a red ribbon. Her features were striking, yet hard, and her upright stance spoke of domination. She was noticeably older than her rivals. "Pray, what do you... *inquisit*?" she asked mockingly.

Unable to contain his mirth, Loxley snorted, as Sophie and Isabel burst into giggles.

"I investigate crimes on behalf of Mr Pepys, Clerk of the Acts for the King's navy," Abby said boldly, causing a hush to descend.

"That is all very well, my dear," said Arabella with a faint smirk. "But there are no crimes here to investigate. Now, shall we play?"

"Abigail!"

Loxley's monkey let out a high-pitched squeal. Abby turned and froze.

The King was approaching.

"Abigail!" he called again, waving cheerfully, though he was scarcely ten yards away.

Sourly, the courtiers muttered.

When Molly darted forward to peck the King on the cheek, he pinched her on the bottom, grinning, but did not break his stride.

Kneeling before Abby, he took her hand and pressed his lips to it. "Mistress Harcourt," he said, his voice warm. "What a pleasure to make your acquaintance once again."

Abby blushed. "The honour is all mine, Your Majesty."

She could feel the hostility radiating from behind her.

"Will you play with us, Charlie?" Arabella asked.

"I would prefer it if she did not," Sophie sneered, her gaze fixed on Abby.

The King rose. As he did so, Loxley's monkey scampered up His Majesty's silken breeches, onto his chest, and snatched at a jewelled clasp on his cravat. Deftly, Charles prised the creature free, holding it at arm's length for the duke to reclaim. "Figaro shares your taste for finery, James. You have trained him well."

"Hand him your riches, and he might make a finer king," Loxley replied, reaching for the monkey.

The King's jaw tightened, but before he could reply, Arabella interjected, "Will you play?"

"In a while," Charles replied, glare fixed on Loxley. "I will speak with Abigail first."

"If you would rather speak with her," Sophie cut in, "then I shall take my leave."

The King turned to Abby, a playful smile on his lips. "If you must," he said, not shifting his dark brown eyes from the inquisitor's.

"Pig!" Sophie spat, her voice trembling with rage, as she stormed off in a flurry of silk and petticoats.

Charles led Abby to one side. While he spoke, the clack of mallet heads striking wooden pall-mall balls echoed about the park.

"Pray, do not be afeared of me, Abigail," he said, taking her hand. "A king is also a gentleman."

He was very tall - almost as tall as Jacob, she realised - and dressed in the finest materials. His periwig fell to his chest, framing his long, solemn face, while three ostrich feathers quivered in the breeze atop his hat. The sleeves of his white shirt spilled from beneath a gold-embroidered burgundy coat, and his high leather boots were polished so assiduously that Abby could see the clouds reflected in them.

His eyes were heavy-lidded, his lips thin, and his nose pronounced. He seemed almost sombre, and certainly no Adonis.

As she studied him, she could think only of his hedonism and extravagance.

The country had welcomed the return of a monarch after the oppression of Cromwell's Commonwealth, and initially, Charles's reign had been celebrated. Yet the tide, Abby knew, was turning. Taxes had risen, while the ongoing war with the Dutch drained resources, and inflation had driven up the cost of basic goods. The mood in the city was becoming increasingly mutinous.

Abby recalled the hated Hearth Tax, introduced by the King to maintain his household. Two shillings per hearth or stove per year, payable into the royal purse. When disgruntled homeowners blocked up their chimneys in protest, they were charged double.

The King regarded her, perplexed. "Spare me your thoughts, Abigail," he said. "I see fire in those exquisite eyes of yours."

"I was remembering all your kindly acts as our King, Your Majesty," she replied. "You are truly adored throughout the land."

He squeezed her hand. "But am I adored by you?"

Her head began to swim. "As any loyal subject loves her king."

A wry smile curled on his lips. "My friend, Mr Pepys, is a fine judge of character." Rolling his shoulders, he exhaled. "Shall we play pall-mall?"

Abby rubbed her stomach, wincing as if it were tender. "I fear the rich dinner fare has given me a turn, Your Majesty. I am unaccustomed to it. If it pleases you, I will return to my lodgings to rest."

The King tilted his head. "Do you deny me?"

Abby's mouth opened and closed.

Releasing her hand, he burst into laughter. "Your face is a picture, Abigail! I assure you, I would not detain you here at court if your heart lies elsewhere. As you can see, I have distractions aplenty. Since I owe you a debt of gratitude – my life, indeed – you may come and go as you please." Snapping his fingers, he called into the air, "Bring a sedan chair! And quickly!"

Chapter Nine

The Earl of Lindsey

*M*argaret Standish sighed petulantly, twisting, as her maid helped her into her stays. "He will not do at all, Elspeth."

Elspeth, who knew better than to reply to her young mistress, murmured an affirmation.

"His father fought on the side of King Charles, loyal to the Crown," Margaret continued. "His family's lands were stripped away, and they've been marked by Cromwell ever since. The Berties may still bear their title, but their power is sorely diminished. At least Father had the sense to side with the Lord Protector."

The maid, behind her, tugging on the laces, nodded silently.

"I dare say the Berties desire our influence far more than we seek theirs," Margaret added.

"Is that comfortable, Mistress Margaret?"

"Their estate lies in Lincolnshire, for pity's sake, Elspeth! I would sooner die than live there!"

"Indeed, mistress. Shall I fetch your petticoats?"

"Mmm." Catching sight of herself in a looking glass, Margaret tilted her face downwards and primped her blonde curls. "I dread to meet the man. What if he resembles a farmer?"

Margaret, now 16, had been allocated her own private chamber in Standish Hall. Its walls were hung with rugs from the East, decorated with exotic creatures - tigers, elephants, snakes, birds of paradise - gifted to her father, Sir Miles. His work with the Navy Board and contacts within the East India Company of traders had its uses, she had discovered. Better still, Anne coveted her wall-hangings and was seethingly jealous.

A tall, intricately carved wardrobe housed her gowns, cloaks and shoes; her dressing table, sited in front of a large leaded window, was topped with perfume bottles and jewellery boxes. The room was dominated by a canopied four-poster bed, with plump pillows and fine linen sheets.

She had been up since dawn, preparing for the arrival of her latest suitor, Henry Bertie, Second Earl of Lindsey. Her parents had been furiously match-making of late, and Henry was the latest in line for her withering stare and ultimate rejection.

The title, she craved, but only on her terms.

A tentative knock came on her door. "May I enter?" It was Anne, her youngest sister, aged ten.

"If you must."

Anne stepped inside, wearing a long silk gown in pale blue and a white apron, tied at the waist. Her blonde hair was plaited and secured with a matching bow. Margaret, attending to her jewellery while Elspeth quietly fussed, did not spare her a glance.

"Isn't it thrilling?" Anne asked, taking a seat on the bed. "You look so elegant, Margaret. I'm certain the Earl will be smitten."

Margaret turned to face her sister. "The Earl is an oaf."

Anne gasped. Although she was accustomed to her sister's nature, Margaret's bluntness still had the power to shock.

Before she could reply, their eldest sister, Elizabeth, appeared in the doorway. "Are you both ready?" she asked. "The Earl and his retinue have arrived."

While a flustered Elspeth rearranged her mistress's pearls, Margaret replied, "For all I care, he may return to Lincolnshire."

Elizabeth, who found her sister's attitude tiresome, tutted. "Henry Bertie is a fine match for you, Margaret. His family's estate is vast, and once the King is restored, his position will rise again. You could fare far worse."

Margaret fixed her older sister's gaze. "Indeed. I might be betrothed to Edmund Carter, the wool merchant who reeks of his sheep."

Elizabeth did not rise to the bait, content in the knowledge that her fiancé owned half of Bristol and was a caring soul, if a little rugged. "Hang any more pearls around that slender neck, dear sister, and you will frighten poor Henry away."

"That is precisely my intention."

"Then your arrogance will leave you a spinster."

"You're just jealous because you settled for less."

Elizabeth's lips narrowed as she turned on her heel and fled. Anne, still perched on the bed, watched intently as Margaret dabbed perfume onto her wrists.

Margaret swivelled sharply in her chair. "Leave me be, child!" she said curtly.

The following morning at breakfast, the three sisters, Jacob and their mother ate in strained silence. Sir Miles had left earlier, taking the twins, James and Robert, to Greenwich docks where they were being trained as midshipmen. England was at war with Spain once again, and Cromwell demanded sacrifice and loyalty.

Sir Miles had been glad to take his leave. The previous day's garden party had not gone to plan.

"It was dreadful, Mother," said Elizabeth, tearing into a roll. "Poor Henry…"

"Poor Henry offered me lilies, Mother!" Margaret interjected. "He thought flowers could woo me!"

Lady Standish had heard it all before. "Lilies?" she replied absent-mindedly, her finger lightly tracing the rim of her teacup.

"Aye, lilies - for funerals!" Margaret exclaimed. "I could hardly contain myself."

"As I recall it, you did not," her older sister cut in.

"Why can you not behave more like your sister?" Lady Standish asked Margaret, her tone heavy with resignation. "It

would please us greatly. After all, we wish only the best for you and ask little in return."

Anne caught Jacob's eye as he selected fruit from a bowl and winked at him. Distracted, he fumbled an apple, and it rolled across the table.

Lady Standish's thick brown eyebrows knotted. "Must you fail at even the simplest of tasks, Jacob?" she said tersely. "Perhaps if you paid more attention, you would not be a constant embarrassment to us."

Mumbling an apology, he retrieved the apple and replaced it in the bowl. Anne, he noticed, was sticking her tongue out at him.

Lady Standish returned her attention to her middle daughter. "I trust one day we will find you a suitor who meets with your approval as well as ours," she said. "Your handsomeness is plain for all to see, if only your tongue were half as beguiling."

"Am I handsome?" Anne piped up.

Margaret snorted.

Anne ignored her. "One day I shall marry a dashing prince and live in his grand castle."

"Aye," replied Margaret with a bitter laugh. "The day that pigs sprout wings."

"Be silent!" Lady Standish commanded, slamming her knife handle into the table.

Elizabeth leaned toward Anne. "Be careful what you wish for, little sister. Your features are indeed handsome and one day you will have your choice of men. But beauty fades and once a man sees past it, what then remains? There is more to life than mere looks."

"But it serves Margaret well enough," Anne countered. "Men fawn over her, while she so carelessly discards them."

"Anne dreams of her own prince," scoffed Margaret, her mouth full of bread. "But she will never match me."

Anne puffed out her cheeks, glaring. "I would not wish to match you, Margaret. One day, mark my words, I will best you."

Jacob could only watch in silence; even Margaret, for once, was lost for words.

Chapter Ten

Reconciliation

Anne Standish was preparing for the pall-mall tournament with the other mistresses when a hesitant rap came at her door. Twenty years old, she had been at court for almost a year and a half, and was confident of her place there - until the insolent Molly Tanner had appeared, that is. The arrogant harlot, a year her junior, had a tongue filthier than a butcher's alley. As if that were not enough, Hakewill, the meddling snake, had seen fit to move her into the lodgings next door.

Scowling to herself, she replaced the comb on her dresser and went to unlock the door.

"Jacob!" she gasped, stepping back in shock. "What brings you here?"

When he moved to embrace her, she retreated further. "Is something wrong?" he asked.

Blinking, she stood aside and beckoned him to enter. "Nay," she said quickly. "Nay, nought! Enter, pray.

You're always welcome. 'Tis just… I was not expecting you."

"What a grand apartment," he said, his eyes darting about the room.

Plush velvet curtains framed tall, arched windows, allowing the afternoon's overcast light to play upon the surfaces within. Tapestries and portraits adorned the walls - there, a painting of the King looking mighty pleased with himself, and next to it, one of his sister Anne, smiling demurely, her blonde hair styled in wispy ringlets.

"I sat for Peter Lely, Charlie's favourite painter," Anne said, noticing Jacob's curiosity.

He stared at his sister, agog. "You refer to His Majesty as… *Charlie*?" he squeaked.

She giggled. "We all do," she said.

She has changed since last we met, he thought. Anne's face was thinner, harder, and she carried herself differently. Her chin was higher, her back straighter.

"Sit," she said, motioning to one of the sumptuously upholstered chairs arranged around a heavy oak table at the centre of the room. The table was strewn with trinkets - gold and silver necklaces, jewelled brooches, strings of pearls - piled carelessly, as if Anne had run out of space to store her treasures. The flickering candlelight from an ornate silver candlestick at the centre made the precious metals glow.

Against one wall stood a harpsichord with ivory keys and meticulous inlaid decoration. The air smelled of luxury – a blend of lavender and rosewater, perfumes shipped from distant, exotic lands at the King's command. Every detail proclaimed wealth and power.

Anne, Jacob realised, shaking his head in admiration, had achieved her ambition.

"Are you happy?" he asked.

She wrinkled her nose. "What a curious question. Indeed, I am, Jacob." She paused, a hint of smugness on her lips. "Perfectly, exquisitely contented."

"Yet you lock yourself in."

Her lips pursed and she picked up a fistful of treasures from the table. "See this?" she said. "'Tis but a fraction of the King's gifts. I dare not leave my door unlocked. Would you?"

Jacob reached for her hand, and she pulled it away. "Forgive me," he said. "I wish only for your happiness."

They talked awhile, the conversation rarely straying from Anne and her life in the royal household. She described a life of wanton leisure – tennis, bowling, pall-mall, visits to the theatre, the horse racing and the King's menagerie at the Tower – in tones of practised delight.

"Does His Majesty treat you kindly?" he asked.

"Why, Charlie is a perfect gentleman. To us all."

"The King's many mistresses?"

Anne's dainty nostrils flared. "'Tis his royal prerogative. Naturally," she added, "I remain his favourite."

"As we entered the palace, we chanced upon Molly Tanner…" he began innocently.

Anne rose abruptly, fists clenched. "Speak not of that errant whore! She…" Jacob's sister caught herself, drew a breath, and sat down. With a forced smile, she concluded, "She delights me not."

"Then the mistresses are at daggers?"

She reached across and took his hand, laughing unconvincingly. "There are tensions, which is only natural, but mostly we are firm friends. 'Tis what Charlie desires. There is room enough at his court for us all."

Jacob placed his other hand over hers, squeezing gently. "Your privy?" he asked.

The staircase was lined with portraits in thick gilt frames, depicting men and women adorned with jewelled crowns and fur-edged gowns of gold and deep red. The King's ancestors, Jacob surmised, though he could name not one.

At the top of the stairs, a long corridor stretched out before him, illuminated by candles on silver sconces. At the far end, Anne had told him, was the privy. Yet several doors lined the hallway, and he longed to delve further into his little sister's enviable new life.

The first door on his left, Jacob noticed, was slightly ajar.

As he cautiously pushed it open, it creaked, and he cast a furtive glance back down the stairs. Inside was a four-poster bed, its coverings piled haphazardly in the centre of the mattress, a dressing table strewn with bottles, jars, and jewellery, a large, studded trunk, a bedside table cluttered with papers, and a pair of plush chairs. He immediately recognised the wall hangings as having once belonged to his sister, Margaret: those rugs decorated with exotic creatures, which Anne had always hankered after.

Then he noticed the floor, strewn with clothing, and there, against the wall, three cages, side by side. In one, an unmoving ball of cream-tipped dark spines, and in the others, brown rodents clambering over one another.

"Beware the snake!"

Jacob jumped.

The inhuman, harsh voice was followed by a raucous shriek, and Jacob slammed the door shut. As he did so, he noticed a large bell-shaped object hanging from a rafter, covered in a black cloth. That was where the devil's words had come from, he felt certain.

"What are you doing?" His sister was standing at the foot of the staircase, glaring up at him.

"What was…"

"'That is *my chamber*, Jacob," she cut in through gritted teeth. "A lady's private business."

"That voice, it…"

"'Tis my parrot, you fool."

"Parrots can speak?" he asked incredulously.

"Only the rarest. I can have anything I desire here, Jacob. His Majesty is a most generous benefactor."

"The bird… It told me to beware the snake…?"

"It warns me of you, you fool, meddling in my chamber, uninvited."

Sheepishly, Jacob began descending the stairs. "Does the King lay with you there? Beside the… parrot?"

Anne tutted loudly. "Does it appear as though he does? This house is mine and mine alone."

"*You keep mice!*" he blurted out. "For why?"

Anne's expression turned dark, then softened. Jacob was standing before her when she finally replied. "I love all God's creatures, Jacob. The mice are my pets. Don't you adore them?"

"Nay," he said. "Nay, I do not."

Turning on her heel, Anne reached for her coat, which was lying over the back of a chair. "I'm late for the pall-mall tournament," she said brusquely.

He stood awkwardly, fiddling with his periwig. "Well, 'twas a pleasure to see you."

She pulled on a pair of soft leather gloves. "I neglected to ask what it is you do these days. Still obeying Father's every whim in the navy? Apprentice carpenter, was it?"

She knew full well what his post had been. "Purser, Anne. Apprentice purser," he replied. "But I have a new purpose now."

"Were you dismissed?"

"In truth, aye, I was. But 'twas a stroke of good fortune," Jacob added eagerly, "since I now work for a most distinguished gentleman by the name of Samuel Pepys, who is Clerk of the Acts to the Navy Board. He worked with our father and advises the King. You may have heard of him?"

"And what are your duties for this marvellous Mr Pepys?"

"I am his inquisitor."

Anne shook her head, perplexed.

"I investigate nefarious dealings on his behalf," Jacob explained.

"I'm late for the King," she said. "You should leave."

Chapter Eleven

Rude Awakenings

Abby awoke to a frantic cry from the courtyard outside: "*Mistress de Valois est morte! Mistress de Valois est morte!*"

Jacob, who had been asleep on the same landing, rushed into her room dressed in a long cotton night-shirt. The air in there smelled of bergamot and lavender. "Do you hear it?" he asked.

"Indeed, Jacob," she replied, rubbing her eyes and swinging her legs over the edge of the bed. It had been the soundest night's sleep she had ever experienced, snuggled in all those luxurious fabrics, and she had not wanted it to end - least of all, with news of that dreadful French woman.

"What is he saying?" Jacob asked.

"He's saying that Sophie de Valois is dead."

Jacob clasped his face with both hands. "Such terrible news!" He paused. "Who is she?"

"One of the King's mistresses." Abby yawned. "I met them yesterday in the park. Sophie is… was the French one with the sour disposition and a ready sneer."

"She sounds awful."

Abby yawned, stretching her arms high above her head. "Wait till you meet Arabella Wyndham. When I told her I act as Mr Pepys's inquisitor, she replied," Abby mimicked Arabella's mocking tone, "Pray, what do you… *inquisit?*' They all laughed at me."

Jacob was horrified. "But…" he spluttered. "How dare she? I shall confront the harlot and rebuke her for such impertinence."

Abby shook her head, smiling, warmed by his defence.

"You do not seem troubled by this French lady's death?" he asked.

"Death is a way of life in this city, Jacob. I'll not be mourning her."

"What if she died in suspicious circumstances? As Mr Pepys's personal inquisitors, we are surely compelled to investigate?"

Abby's bleary eyes sprang open, and she sighed as the truth of his words hit her. She had planned to leave court that very day, to return to her lodgings on Seething Lane, away from all the fakery and splendour of the court. *Now I may be trapped here*, she thought.

It was loyalty to Pepys alone that dragged her from her bed that morning.

Out in the courtyard, she questioned the Frenchman who had so rudely woken them.

When she returned inside, the maid, Betsy, was laying out breakfast: cold venison pie, crusty rolls, English cheeses, butter and a platter of fruit. Everything freshly baked in the palace's Great Bakehouse.

Jacob was already tucking in. "What did he say?"

Taking the chair opposite, she sucked on her lower lip. "Mistress de Valois was struck down, it seems, by a falling chandelier."

"An accident?"

"Unlikely, Jacob. How many chandeliers simply fall from their rafters? And in a royal palace, to boot?"

Jacob looked up at their own ceiling and its dark oak beams. "Many of these buildings are old, as well you know. We should visit the scene of the lady's demise ourselves."

Must we? she thought, just as the door flew open and a breathless Pepys appeared, clutching his hat lest it tumble in his haste.

"Have you heard the news?" he asked. "Mistress de Valois is dead. Such sorrowful tidings."

Jacob stood and bowed. "We have, sir. Should we hasten to the good lady's aid?"

Eyeing the table laden with food, Pepys rubbed his hands in anticipation. "Perhaps a light breakfast first, as

I have not had mine. Mistress de Valois, I am sure, will wait."

"Since she is dead?" Abby asked.

Pepys peered at her. "Aye, Abigail Harcourt. Since she is dead."

While Betsy replenished the platters, he told them Sophie de Valois's story.

Three and some years ago, she had arrived in England as the niece of Philippe de Valois, a minor courtier to King Louis XIV of France. Sophie had been plucked from obscurity, chosen for her wit and beauty, to inveigle herself into King Charles's court. She was presented to the King at a lavish reception at the French Embassy in London. "And in a trice, His Highness was smitten," said Pepys.

To the French, she was a planted insider, subtly steering English foreign policy in their favour. To the English, her presence was a means to alleviate diplomatic tensions, particularly as King Louis paid Charles a handsome sum to secure the arrangement.

Abby puffed out her cheeks. "Molly Tanner told me she spies for the French."

"Already your inquisitor's instincts are at play," said Pepys. "I congratulate you."

Molly had offered the information unbidden; Abby played along, smiling coyly.

"I know something of Mistress de Valois's dealings myself, but am sworn to secrecy," said Pepys. "Sir William Hakewill may be less guarded. I suggest you both meet with him at the earliest opportunity."

"I am keen to see the unfortunate lady's body, sir," said Jacob. "We may discover some clue to her murderer."

"We don't know if it is murder," Abby pointed out.

"Chandeliers do not plummet to the floor by themselves, Abigail. Not in the King's palace," said Pepys, pushing away his empty plate. "Shall we depart?"

Chapter Twelve

Foppery

Pepys led the way back towards the Privy Stairs, left past Anne Standish's lodgings and out into the sweeping garden with walkways that Abby had passed through with Molly Tanner. "The Pebble Court," Pepys noted brusquely, before turning sharp left.

At least he knows the way, thought Abby, who was still bamboozled by the multitude of streets and alleyways that seemed to delight in their maze-like turns. Heavy rain was falling from a sky the colour of ash; the tall, enclosed buildings had shielded them from it. Now, out in the open, it battered their skin and dripped from their noses. The wind was up, too.

The two men pulled their hat brims down over their faces. Abigail, who had no head covering, blew the raindrops from her lips. It was a fine day for a murder.

"Have you met with your sister, Jacob?" Pepys asked over the noise of the swirling weather.

"Aye, sir."

Pepys, obliged to press further, added, "How went it?"

"'Twas a joy, sir," Jacob replied curtly.

"Ahead is the Stone Gallery," explained Pepys, as they reached a narrow, flagstone corridor with large, mullioned windows on one side, allowing murky daylight to illuminate its length. "And here," he said, as they emerged into a glorious green space, divided symmetrically into sixteen lawns, each with a marble-and-bronze statue at its centre, "is the Privy Garden."

"'Tis truly a wondrous sight," said Jacob, stunned that such a sweeping, elegant garden could be somehow hidden among so many clustered and crumbling buildings.

Abby rushed ahead, turning left to follow a paved walkway. "Mr Pepys, is this the sundial you once spoke of? 'Tis grander even than you described," she said, reaching a substantial, multi-faceted structure carved from a single block of stone.

Its base was over four feet square, featuring five dials: four at the corners and a larger, concave dial in the centre. This main dial was encircled by four intricate rings, marking the calendar months, zodiac signs, compass directions and the days of each month.

Abby traced the smooth curve of the central dial with her palm, marvelling at its intricate craftsmanship. The central gnomon cast no shadow that morning, with the sun obscured by clouds, but that did not detract from the magnificence of the piece.

"Do not tarry, Abigail!" Pepys called to her. "Already my finest stockings are soaked through!"

Turning, she saw him disappear through a door in the high east wall, followed by Jacob.

"Hold for me!" she called back.

Sir William Hakewill paced up and down before his desk, wheezing, as Pepys and his inquisitors shook the rain from their clothing. Jacob managed to let go of his hat as he swung it in front of the fire; it spun towards the desk and sent an inkwell sprawling.

"Clumsy oaf!" Hakewill grumbled, dabbing at the spreading black puddle with a cloth. "Is this man truly fit for your service, Pepys?"

Pepys shot Jacob a withering look as the inquisitor retrieved his hat. "I would swear by his efficiency, Sir William," he said.

The dark-panelled walls were lined with shelves crammed with neatly ordered ledgers and leather-bound volumes. Otherwise, the room was sparsely adorned, just the King's crest above the fireplace and a map of England on the wall beside the rear door.

"What do you make of it, then, Pepys? The French will be up in arms once news reaches them of Mistress de Valois's death. I fear it may drive a wedge between our two countries, just as relations were healing."

"Was it murder?" Pepys asked, settling into a chair.

Other chairs stood empty; the inquisitors remained standing.

"You tell me, Pepys."

Pepys rubbed his hands together, hoping to create some warmth. "Sir, I request that my inquisitors visit the site of the… incident. And that they are granted access to Mistress de Valois's body."

Hakewill perched on the edge of his desk. Devoid of his periwig, tufts of wispy grey hair could be seen sprouting in odd places.

Stroking his chin, he spoke in a sombre tone. "The King would prefer it if the matter simply disappeared."

"But it will not, Sir William," Pepys pointed out.

"How is the King?" Jacob piped up.

Hakewill stared at him. "Why? Is he a friend of yours?"

Shaking his head, Pepys closed his eyes. When he opened them, Jacob was still there.

Saving Jacob's further blushes, Abby spoke up. "How has His Majesty taken Mistress de Valois's death?"

The King's adviser turned his sights on Abby. "How do you imagine His Majesty would have taken her death?" he asked.

"I'm not sure he cared much for her," she replied. "Nor, I believe, did you, Sir William."

Hakewill's eyes widened. *The insolence of the girl!*

Pepys rose to his feet, stammering, "I… I… I assure you…"

Hakewill raised his hand for silence.

Jacob glanced nervously at Abby, whose cheeks had flushed crimson.

"I would have this young lady banished from the court, Pepys," Hakewill said. "She has the tongue of a devil and the cheek of a beggar."

When Pepys tried to interject, Hakewill continued, "However. We must handle this with due diligence or risk the wrath of our French allies. Mr Pepys, since you assure me that your inquisitors are the best in the land…" Abby and Jacob exchanged raised eyebrows as Hakewill went on, "I shall permit their investigation."

Pepys bowed. "And they will not disappoint His Majesty, I assure…"

Once again, Hakewill spoke over him, "'Tis not the King who desires this investigation, but I. As I told you, His Majesty would rather draw a veil over the whole sorry matter. Sadly, even for he, that will not be possible."

Abby spoke. "He is not alarmed by Sophie's death?"

"His Majesty prefers a life untroubled by… irksome details."

Mistress de Valois's death - an irksome detail? thought Abby, but she held her tongue.

Keen to display his competence, Jacob asked, "We heard tell, Sir William, that she spied for the French?"

"I told him nought, sir!" Pepys cut in.

"'Twas common knowledge, Pepys," Hakewill replied, and paused, clearly caught in two minds. "Less common knowledge, is that she spied also for us."

"She played both sides!" cried Jacob. "Fie, sir!"

"And most ineptly, Mr Standish. Too easily were her deceits revealed."

"How so?" Jacob asked, as Pepys and Abby also pricked up their ears.

Hakewill retrieved a clay pipe and taper from his desk, walked to the fireplace, lit the taper in the flames and applied it to the pipe bowl. Once the tobacco caught, he stood warming his back, releasing clouds of smoke toward the ceiling. It was apparent that he enjoyed the attention.

"There was once a diplomatic incident 'twixt England and France, which might well have ended in war," he said.

"What was the cause?" Jacob asked.

"King Louis accused His Majesty of referring to him," he paused for effect, "as a fop."

"What was the source of this scurrilous rumour?" Jacob asked.

"'Twas hardly scurrilous, Mr Standish, for the French King is indeed a fop. However, we would not wish it known that the King views him as such - and yet he did, in a letter to Mistress de Valois."

"You suspect she passed on the letter?" Abby asked. "The rumour may surely have come from another source?"

"Indeed. And that is why we devised a false letter for the French whore, in which His Majesty expressed a desire for a new creature for his menagerie. When the French ambassador next visited court, he brought with him a python - which promptly escaped. Thus, we had our culprit, Mistress Harcourt."

"Her actions might have caused a war betwixt our nations," Pepys piped up. "I am surprised His Majesty forgave her."

Hakewill tapped the table. "Who's to say that he did?"

Abby stroked a damp strand of red hair from her eye. "You consider the King's mistresses to be of lowly status, Sir William, and a drain on the royal purse. Yet he delights in their company and could scarcely live without them. It might be argued that they earn their keep."

Hakewill snarled as he flung his pipe into the fire. "I earn my keep a thousand times more justly than those harlots - yet the King neglects to pay *me*!"

With that, he strode towards the rear door of his study, deliberately treading on Jacob's toe as he did so. "Keep your inquisitor in check, Mr Pepys - I hold you responsible. Now, begone! My time is precious. I suggest you visit the Vane Room, where Mistress de Valois met her end."

Hakewill stood in the doorway, watching as Pepys and his inquisitors made their way out.

"What of the mistress's body, sir?" Jacob asked, peering behind the adviser, into what appeared to be a living space.

Noticing it, Hakewill quickly slammed the door behind him. "You will need the King's permission to see it," came his muffled reply.

Chapter Thirteen

Sir Arthur Neville

*S*ir Arthur Neville was a powerful court diplomat, tasked with managing trade negotiations and maintaining diplomatic relations with European powers - a crucial role in the wake of England's interminable wars and emerging global influence. His estate, a sprawling property in Hertfordshire, served as both a country retreat and a venue for political gatherings.

A skilled courtier with ties to naval interests, he hosted lavish parties where he sought to increase his own influence by introducing promising young figures to the circles of power. Though dull in personality, Sir Arthur's connections to the King's Privy Council and his foreign ties made him a valuable ally.

So it was not for the food and music that Sir Miles Standish escorted his daughter, Anne, to one of Sir Arthur's parties in November 1664. If he could inveigle her into the strongholds of English power, it foretold riches and influence for both, and kudos for Sir Arthur - everyone would be a winner.

The banqueting hall that night radiated warmth and wealth. Tall, mullioned windows framed the falling snow outside, their glass misted with condensation. A fire blazed in the grand hearth, its smoky aroma mingling with the cloying scent of spiced wine, filling the air with a heady sense of the impending Christmas season.

In one corner, musicians played a joyful air on lute, viol, and recorder, each casting the occasional glance at the scene before them, striving to conceal their envy.

A vast rectangular table dominated the centre of the room. Around it were seated two dozen or so guests on stately chairs, exquisitely crafted. The table was draped in heavy velvet, embroidered with glittering thread. Silver platters laden with roasted meats and glazed winter vegetables reflected the flickering light of the candelabras overhead.

The guests, dressed in sumptuous silks, velvets and brocades, feasted, the low murmur and occasional outburst of their conversations echoing about the hall.

Anne found herself seated at the far end, between Sir Arthur at the head of the table - Sir Miles having pulled a few strings - and a senior Whitehall clerk named Edmund Pierce, to her left. Her father, opposite and a few seats along, caught her attention every now and again, nodding furtively to chivvy her along.

She needed no telling. The opportunity to mingle with the kingdom's most powerful men came only rarely, even with her father's influence, and Anne was determined not to squander it. Smoothed discourse in the right ear, and the rewards might be magnificent.

Quickly, however, she realised that gaining Sir Arthur's attention would not be easy. A large man with a boundless appetite and bellowing laugh, he was engrossed in talk of trade with a foreign ambassador to his right and would not be distracted from it.

Pierce nudged Anne with his elbow and spoke in a low voice. "'Tis a wonder anybody can hear themselves think over Sir Arthur's laughter."

Having ignored him in favour of trying to interrupt their host, Anne found herself staring into the clerk's face. In his late twenties, he had prominent cheekbones, cropped black hair and an intelligent gaze that transfixed her. She blinked. "You are, sir?"

Pierce introduced himself. "And you are Anne Standish, daughter of the esteemed Navy Board Surveyor, Sir Miles Standish."

Anne pulled back, an amused smile playing on her lips. "You know my name."

"'Tis my duty to know people's names – and their business," Pierce replied.

"And what is my business, Mr Pierce?" she asked.

He merely smiled.

Warming to his game, Anne leaned in closer. "Sir Arthur does seem rather pleased with himself."

"Or perhaps ensuring the ambassador cannot get a word in edgewise?"

Anne's fair eyebrow arched. "You think him cunning?"

"I think him careful, as any man in his position should be. He knows the stake in every conversation."

Anne gave a small laugh. "And what of you, sir? Are you careful?"

His smile widened, eyes glinting. "I prefer to think of myself as… strategically aware."

Anne tilted her head. "And what strategy do you employ at a party such as this?"

Pierce glanced toward Sir Arthur, then back at her. "The best strategy, Mistress Standish, is to know when to speak and when to listen. Most men here are too eager to hear their own voices." Pausing, he flicked a flake of ash off his black doublet and added smoothly, "However, when one is seated beside a lady as handsome as yourself, then…"

"Mistress Standish! Forgive me my impertinence!" With the foreign ambassador making his way from the hall, Sir Arthur had finally turned his attention to Anne. His voice was thick and gravelly, the sound of mill wheels grinding.

She swivelled to address him, leaving Pierce whispering sweet nothings to the air.

"Sir Arthur, I can but thank you for inviting me to this," she gazed about the hall, shaking her head in wonderment, "most opulent gathering. I am honoured, sir."

Sir Arthur cleared his throat, flushed of face and quite drunk. "I assure you, Mistress Standish, the honour is all mine." He reached for her hand, and as she offered it, he kissed her fingers, his gaze never leaving hers.

As Anne reclaimed her hand, she noticed he had left a red-wine stain behind and wiped it surreptitiously on her gown.

Gazing at Sir Arthur with a fixed grin, she willed herself to find some interesting nugget of discourse. Flustered, she could not, and was obliged to repeat herself. "Your generosity is most gracious. A gathering such as this is truly a spectacle, and one I am privileged to attend."

Happily, Sir Arthur was not immune to repetitive toad-ying. "Aye, indeed!" he bellowed. "I do pride myself on such matters. I believe 'tis in gatherings such as this that a man's influence is most keenly felt."

Sensing her opportunity, Anne struck. "Influence is every-thing, is it not, Sir Arthur? My father, Sir Miles, tells me you have the King's ear, and have introduced many - such as myself - to his court at Whitehall." How dearly she wished her sister, Margaret, could witness her subtle manoeuvrings, captivating these fabulously rich men in their den.

Sucking the meat from a pork knuckle, Sir Arthur tossed the bone behind him, narrowly missing a lute player. "Do you hunt, Mistress Standish?" he asked.

Nay, I do not hunt, *she thought.* "Nay, sir, I have not had the pleasure."

Grunting, Sir Arthur wiped his fingers on the tablecloth. "You must try it some time. There is nought quite like the thrill of the chase."

She tried again. "I find I prefer a quite different thrill, sir. That of power. The forging of alliances…"

Sir Arthur squinted, thoughtfully rubbing his greasy cheek. "I well recall a wager I placed with Lord Tavistock, of one hundred golden guineas…" he said, then began rambling endlessly about bagging the first stag at his estate, while Tavistock accidentally shot a servant, on the opening day of the season. On and on he went, lost in an inebriated haze of self-admiration.

Her father had made it sound so easy, charming this great buffoon with her feminine wiles and securing a coveted place at the royal court. As yet another goblet was downed in one, the ruby-red liquid running in rivulets down either side of Sir Arthur's chin, she began to wonder whether she should have asserted herself earlier in the evening.

Anne's eyes misted over during his hunting monologue; as they cleared, she noticed with horror that the foreign ambassador was returning to his seat. At the same time, she became aware that the general hubbub of the hall had become mysteriously diminished.

When the ambassador reached his chair, he did not sit immediately, but bowed extravagantly - not to her, as she first thought, but to someone behind her; she felt the presence.

Suddenly, Sir Arthur was up and out of his seat, stumbling as he knelt, head bowed. "Your Majesty!" he declared. "To what do I owe such an honour?"

Anne froze. The King himself was standing behind her.

She glanced across at her father, who looked barely able to suppress his glee. When she winked at him, he winced and looked away.

"And who is this fine young lady?" It was the King's voice. Did he refer to her?

As Anne turned, her heart raced. Charles was indeed staring straight at her. Her first thought was how imposing he appeared, taller than she had imagined, yet also rather dour of face. Sunken cheeks, a not inconsiderable nose, and a weary look in his eyes. Why, *she thought,* his long face reminds me of my brother, Jacob's.

As she bowed, the King cheerily bade her stand. "I would know your name, dear lady," he said, those tired eyes suddenly twinkling, "for it eludes me - which is greatly remiss."

Beside Anne, Sir Arthur belched.

The King gave a start. "If I have intruded upon your discourse with Sir Arthur," he said, his gaze lingering on her, "then pray forgive me. I would not wish…"

She shook her head, a little over-eagerly. "His Majesty is too gracious. However, our discourse was growing rather tiresome, so I am most grateful for your timely arrival."

Charles beamed; here was a lady he could work with.

Chapter Fourteen

The Vane Room

Outside in the Privy Garden, Pepys made a dash to his right and disappeared through an open doorway in the wall. The weather had, if anything, worsened. So dark were the clouds that the morning felt like nighttime, and thunder could be heard in the distance. The rain battered down as if it might never stop.

Abby looked up at Jacob, pursed her lips, and followed her employer.

"What say you, inquisitors?" Pepys asked as they sheltered at the foot of a stone stairway.

"That the King cares little for Sophie's death, and that Hakewill positively gloats over it," Abby replied.

Pepys clamped his hand over her mouth, leaned close and said quietly but firmly, "I have told you before, Abigail, the walls have ears! We are surrounded here by council offices. Decry His Majesty at your peril."

Jacob leaned down until his face was close to theirs, forming an awkwardly intimate huddle. "Did you see inside Hakewill's apartment?" he asked conspiratorially. "For a gentleman who claims he is not paid, his walls are adorned with very many paintings."

Pepys pulled back, scowling. "You forget, Jacob, that Hakewill is not only the Lord High Treasurer but also nephew to the Earl of Essex, who owns Britain's finest collection of Van Dyck portraits. Ties to such wealth bring privileges." He paused. "Only last month, Hakewill's own likeness was painted by none other than Peter Lely."

"The King's favoured portrait artist," said Jacob. "He lately painted my sister."

Pepys sighed. "Mr Lely paints all the King's mistresses, Jacob. 'Tis a perk of the… position."

"Might one of the mistresses have murdered Sophie?" Abby asked. "There is no love lost 'twixt them all."

Pepys pursed his lips. "We must first determine whether foul play was indeed at work."

"Then we must visit the scene of the crime, sir," said Jacob.

"Follow me," said Pepys, setting off up the stairway. "The Vane Room, where Mistress de Valois met her untimely demise, is at the far end of the Privy Gallery atop these stairs."

Having climbed the stone steps, they found themselves facing a door adorned with a magnificent painting of Adam and Eve. The long, stone Privy Gallery stretched out in either direction. "That way lies the Holbein Gate," said Pepys, pointing left. "'Tis this way to the Vane Room," he added, leading them in the opposite direction.

To their left, heavy wooden doors lined the gallery; to the right, a succession of windows overlooked the Privy Garden. From this high vantage point, even in the foul weather, the garden appeared lush and opulent.

"This was once the King's withdrawing chamber," said Pepys, opening the door to the Vane Room. "Now 'tis used for chapters of the Order of the Garter and, on occasion, for the King's dining."

"Odd's fish!" Jacob exclaimed as he first set eyes inside the room.

Abby could only gaze in awe.

The walls were so richly gilded that the flickering orange light of the room's many candles seemed to make the space glow. Exquisitely painted panels depicted mythical creatures entwined with flowing foliage, alongside symbolic representations of earth, air, fire, and water, evoking a sense of cosmic grandeur and the vastness of the four corners of the earth.

How the rich and privileged live, Abby thought, shaking herself from her introspection. "Did Mistress de Valois use the Vane Room?" she asked Pepys.

He paused for a moment. "She would have dined here with His Majesty."

The fireplace was cold, and the room was filled with the scent of burning wax. In the centre stood a long wooden table surrounded by heavy oak chairs. At the far end of the table, on the floor, could be seen a scrolled brass candelabra with floral motifs, holding a dozen candles around its perimeter - all extinguished.

Pepys and his inquisitors stood around it in silent contemplation. A thick rope, once holding the chandelier high in place, now lay coiled haphazardly on the floor.

Jacob picked it up, holding it in both hands and pulling, to test its strength. "It seems sturdy," he said.

"Yet it must have failed, to fall upon the good lady," said Pepys.

Jacob moved to the wall, where a deep-red velvet drape obscured the pulley mechanism used to raise and lower the chandelier for lighting purposes. He pulled it aside. The pulley was there, fixed to the wall, apparently undamaged. A short length of rope, tied to an anchor on the wall, lay on the flagstone floor.

Stooping, he picked it up and inspected it. "It looks to have been partially cut," he said. Sniffing at it, he added, "And burned."

Abby and Pepys joined him. Indeed, the ends of the strands were not frayed, which would have suggested age or wear, but appeared cleanly sliced, with a few others blackened.

Jacob inspected the wall around the anchor. Above it, a hole in the plaster was clean and dry, as if recently made. Just above that was a small dark stain. Dabbing at it, an oily black residue transferred to his fingertip.

"Somebody cut partway through the rope," he said. "Then set a candle here in the wall, concealed behind the drape. It burnt through the remaining strands, sending the candelabra tumbling to the floor."

Pepys gripped Jacob's arm with both hands, eyes glinting. "You are becoming a finer inquisitor, Mr Standish, than I might ever have imagined. Then you conclude that Mistress de Valois was murdered?"

Jacob adjusted his periwig, unable to suppress a small grin of pride. "I do, sir."

Abby cleared her throat. "We assume that Sophie was summoned to this room, alone, by her murderer, through some unknown means…"

The two men nodded, Pepys still clutching Jacob's arm.

Abby continued, "Might she not have sat at any one of these chairs?" she pointed out. "Yet 'tis only that one, at the head of the table, which lay 'neath the chandelier. Did the murderer stipulate which chair she took? It seems odd - odder still that she, wilful and indulged, would comply."

Pepys released his grip on Jacob. The three of them stared at the table and its configuration of chairs, then at the chandelier on the floor.

"Ah!" Pepys blurted. "I have it!"

"That chair," he said, pointing at the one Sophie must have taken, "is not usually set at the head of the table. This one," he gestured to a more extravagantly designed chair with a higher back, "is."

"The two chairs have been exchanged?" asked Jacob.

"Aye, Mr Standish. Indeed they have."

"But how could the murderer be certain she'd take that seat, directly 'neath the chandelier?" Abby asked.

Pepys grinned. "Every seat in this room was crafted by English hands - save that one," he said, motioning to the more delicately wrought chair at the table's head, "which was crafted - note the Fleur de Lys - in France. Mistress de Valois would naturally have taken it."

Jacob gasped. "Then the murderer knows her tastes."

"Aye," said Abby. "I'll wager he - or perhaps she - resides in this very court."

Chapter Fifteen

His Majesty

"**M**istress Harcourt! Mr Pepys! And that other fellow!"

Shocked by the sudden outburst, Pepys and his inquisitors turned to see the King standing in the doorway of the Vane Room. His tall frame, flouncy attire and ostentatious periwig were unmistakable.

"Your Majesty!" said Pepys, as the three of them bowed. "To what do we owe this pleasure?"

The King strode purposefully towards them, his gaze alighting upon the bare end of rope still clutched in Jacob's hand. Peering at it, he asked, "Is there some cause for concern?"

Abby cut in before Jacob could reply. "My inquisitor colleague, Mr Jacob Standish, has ascertained that Mistress de Valois was murdered, Your Majesty."

The King stared down at her, a look of puzzled amusement on his face. "Murdered? What utter nonsense. For what possible reason would anybody murder Sophie?"

"For many possible reasons, Your Majesty," she replied. "Mistress de Valois spied for the French, and her attachment to you may have stoked jealousy among the other mistresses." Registering Charles's frown, she ploughed on, "And I believe she was profligate in her spending, which may have angered… certain courtiers."

The King laughed uproariously, took her hand and kissed it, while she could only look on.

"Mr Pepys," the King said, "your fabled inquisitors do indeed live up to their billing! I have not heard such a magnificent tale since," pausing, he stroked his smooth chin. "Why, since I last saw a play by our esteemed Mr Shakespeare."

"But Your Majesty!" Abby snatched the rope from Jacob. "This rope was cut…"

Sensing Abby's frustration, Pepys gestured for her silence. "Your Majesty," he said calmly. "I beseech you, have patience with my inquisitors. Their work is but beginning, and these are merely early theories…"

Charles nodded.

"I understand they are keen to examine the unfortunate Mistress de Valois's body, in the hope of finding further clues," Pepys continued. "If Your Majesty would be so gracious as to grant their humble request?"

The King placed a hand on Pepys's shoulder; both inquisitors noted the bands of gold and precious stone wrapped around the regal fingers. "You are a loyal ally,

Pepys," he said. "Your inquisitors may indeed see my poor Sophie, who lies at rest in the Great Chapel; however, I assure you they will discover nought of consequence."

Pepys bowed, followed by Abby and Jacob.

The King, turning to leave, paused and glanced back at Abby. "Abigail," he said, raising a finger, "when are we to enjoy some leisure together? I trust you are well rested after yesterday's... fleeting malaise?"

Abby sensed all eyes upon her. "I am, Your Majesty. Were it that I had the time, but I sense the urgency of our work here on behalf of Mr Pepys. I would hate to disappoint so loyal a gentleman."

Oh, but she is sharp, thought the King, with a smirk. "Very well," he said, and wafted from the room, leaving behind a faint scent of jasmine and musk.

The three stood in silence, listening as Charles's footsteps echoed along the Privy Gallery, fading in the direction of the Holbein Gate.

Once the sound had disappeared, Jacob exhaled loudly, his eyes wide and his thick eyebrows raised.

"Abigail Harcourt," Pepys said sharply. "You tread a fine line."

Abby shrugged. "If His Majesty's mistresses may sway him as they please, smitten as he is, why shouldn't I do the same?"

Though Pepys shook his head, she noticed a tight smile flicker across his face.

Chapter Sixteen

La Morte Part I

With Pepys in the lead, the trio retraced their steps, back through the Privy Garden and Pebble Court, past the lodgings of Anne Standish and Molly Tanner. Abby and Jacob felt they might at last be familiarising themselves with the layout of the sprawling palace.

Behind Molly's house, they came upon the Great Chapel. The towering stone edifice bore tall stained-glass windows. Its lead-covered pitched roof was divided into panels, with bosses at the intersections. To banish evil spirits, carved gargoyles and grotesques lined the parapets.

Under the grey sky and the teeming heavens, lit by the occasional flash of lightning, the effect was breathtaking and disturbing in equal measure.

"Come!" said Pepys, clutching his hat to his head and dashing for the door. He was no natural runner, the inquisitors noted of his bustling gait.

Inside was a marvellously high ceiling, panelled and decorated with gold leaf and religious carvings. Bench seating lined the walls on either side, above which ran parallel galleries bearing individual closets separated by decorative hangings.

The trio shook themselves down, leaving puddles on the stone floor.

"His Majesty's closet," said Pepys, pointing to curtained area at the far end of the chapel, shrouded in a heavy, deep-red drape.

Set before it was a raised chancel. There, standing to attention beside a wooden coffin set upon a table, was a single guard clutching an upright halberd.

"How do you do?" Pepys called out, the words echoing disconcertingly about the chamber. Noting the guard's blue-and-gold sash, he told his inquisitors *sotto voce*, "I believe he may be French."

The guard said nothing as they approached up the nave, but merely stared.

When they reached him, they saw that part of his right ear was missing. He wore a green fitted doublet with gilded embroidery, slashed sleeves, and matching breeches. His long, curly hair was the colour of sand.

Abby and Jacob both stole a glance into the coffin behind him. It was Jacob's first view of the King's French mistress, though Abby already knew her face, now stilled, eyelids veiling that once disdainful gaze.

Pepys cleared his throat, breaking the silence. "We are here to pay our respects to Mistress de Valois," he said. "With the permission of His Majesty, King Charles. I am Mr Samuel Pepys, Clerk of the Acts to the Navy Board, and these are my inquisitors, Mr Jacob Standish and Mistress Abigail Harcourt."

The guard's gaze shifted from one to the other. Then, with an almost imperceptible nod, he stepped aside, allowing the trio to draw closer to the coffin.

Jacob's eyes lingered on Sophie's face, serene in death. The elegant curve of her pale lips, the finely arched brows and dainty, upturned nose - features that had captured the King's interest and stoked rivalries. Now frozen in time.

Abby exhaled softly, her mind racing.

Sophie was wearing a white linen shift beneath a burgundy gown with flared sleeves. Her kid-leather gloves suggested she had dressed against the cold.

"At what hour was Mistress de Valois's body discovered?" Abby asked the guard.

After a pause, during which it seemed he either did not understand her or was unwilling to answer, he replied, "Tôt ce matin."

She looked to Pepys, who spoke the language far more adeptly than her, thanks to his French wife. Abby, who merely dabbled, knew "ce matin" as "this morning", but that first word eluded her.

"Early this morning," Pepys dutifully translated.

Addressing the guard once again, she asked, "Was she dressed in this same garb?"

Frowning, he replied in a thick French accent, "I beg your pardon?"

"Leave this to me," said Pepys, and began speaking with the guard in the foreign tongue.

Conversation concluded, Pepys explained that Mistress de Valois had been discovered by one of the King's patrolling yeomen at around four in the morning, in the Vane Room beside the fallen chandelier. "Elle était morte," he added in the guard's original French, which even Jacob appeared to understand.

The King had been woken and informed, and had ordered that her body be taken directly to the Great Chapel. She was indeed wearing the same outfit she had died in.

"Would you ask him if we may inspect the body?" Abby asked Pepys in a whisper. The chapel's overwhelming, stoic silence and insistent echo made her feel self-conscious.

Some negotiation was involved, the guard's voice occasionally shrill as the exchange clearly struck the Frenchman's nerve.

"Merci, monsieur," Pepys concluded at length, then turned to his inquisitors. "He is not best pleased, but has agreed that we may proceed, on the condition that we do not touch Mistress de Valois's face."

Abby blinked back a sudden sadness. *Respect for the dead*, she thought. *Why have I been so heartless?* Sophie de Valois had seemed aggressive and aloof during their brief encounter, yet Abby realised she had simply been protecting her own interests, as any woman might. *I don't know her,* she realised, *and who am I to judge?*

The three men watched - Pepys and Jacob with intrigue, the guard warily - as Abby reached into the coffin and began gently feeling around and beneath the body. Satisfied that no clue was there, she removed Sophie's leather shoes - also empty - and began on the hem of her velvet gown.

"What do you seek?" Jacob asked.

"Anything unusual," she replied. "Sometimes I secrete small items in the hems of my clothing, where others seldom look."

"Aye!" he said, loudly enough that it felt sacrilegious in the holy space, then lowered his voice. "My sisters did the same."

Abby sighed. "Nought," she said, moving to the hem of Sophie's cuff.

When the right cuff proved empty, she switched to the left, but the guard was growing impatient. "Ça suffit," he growled, banging the staff of his halberd into the stone floor.

"Un moment, s'il vous plaît," she replied, holding up a hand.

"Non!" the guard snapped. *"Ça suffit!"*

"Hold!" she hissed. "There's something here."

Tucked inside Mistress de Valois's left cuff was a tatty piece of paper, browned with age. The top right corner was missing, ripped away. Though Abby searched the cuff again, the missing piece was not there.

The guard snatched it from her, holding it up for all to see.

Sir
Deliver th
the utmost dis
lady I did mentio
await me at midnig
Vane Room.
Trust none but her.
Yours in confidence
Samuel Pepys

"What is zis?" the guard demanded, thickly accented. "'Await me at midnight… Vane Room?' 'Yours in confidence, Samuel Pepys?'" He glared at Pepys, who snatched the paper from him with a quivering hand, his face growing pale.

"I… I do not…" he stammered.

"Mr Pepys, did you pen this note?" Abby asked, the query catching in her throat.

"Well, 'tis in my hand." He rubbed his eyes vigorously. "I… I… do recall clandestine meetings with Mistress de Valois, she was…"

"À l'aide!" the guard called out. *"À l'aide!"*

Pepys thrust the paper at him. "But, sir, this note was penned many a year since, it…"

From a door to one side of the chancel, two more French guards came running with swords drawn.

"Emmenez-le!" the original guard commanded, clutching a fistful of Pepys's coat. The inquisitors' esteemed employer suddenly looked very small, like a frightened child.

Jacob moved to intervene, but Abby pulled him back. "Not now," she said sharply.

As Pepys was manhandled up the nave, a guard on each arm and the other at his back with halberd poised, he called back, "Inform His Majesty, Mr Standish! He will not stand for this!" He sounded more desperate than assured.

"Aye, sir! Fear not - we shall soon right this grievous injustice!"

As the door to the Great Chapel slammed shut, Abby and Jacob were enveloped in a fearful silence.

Immediately, Abby pulled a quill, ink and notebook from her satchel and fell to the floor scribbling.

"What are you doing?" Jacob asked.

"Making a copy of that note while I remember it."

"What did it mean?"

"I don't know, Jacob. I wish I did. I do know there's foul play at work here."

Jacob returned his attention to the coffin. "There was something else," he said.

Chapter Seventeen

The Ring

May 1665.

Standish Hall's banqueting hall had been festooned with fresh garlands of ivy and roses, all arranged under the beady eye of Lady Honoria. The high, vaulted ceiling was hung with naval banners, while the Standish family crest took pride of place over the huge fireplace. Servants hurried back and forth, preparing the three long tables that dominated the centre of the room.

Sir Miles's youngest daughter, Anne, was about to enter the court of King Charles, and he was determined that this celebration would become the focus of noble gossip. Moving through the hall with purpose, dressed in his finest brocaded doublet, ceremonial sword at his side, he stopped at a small table by the window.

Upon it lay a pair of miniature oval portraits: his twin sons, Robert and James, in their naval uniforms, gazing defiantly into the future. Sir Miles picked them up, one in each hand, and lowered his head. His sons had no future now. The young lieutenants had perished side by side, as they would have wished, at the Battle of Lowestoft during the Second Dutch War. A finely detailed wooden model of their third-rate ship of the line, HMS Lionheart, stood beside the portraits.

Sir Miles had learned of their loss only a week ago, yet he was resolute that the tragedy would not overshadow the festivities. This small commemorative display would afford the brave young men a presence at the event. Now only Jacob remained, he was all too aware, as his sole surviving heir.

He had faith in the lad, he assured himself. Having secured Jacob a position as an apprentice purser, Sir Miles had ensured he would continue to uphold the family tradition of loyal naval service. He would make a gentleman of his youngest son yet.

Replacing the portraits, his hand moved to the silk pocket inside his doublet, feeling for its contents. Still there, he reassured himself, tracing the outline with his fingers.

"Miles!" His wife was calling to him.

There she was, hands on hips in the doorway, wearing the magnificently fashionable silk gown he had brought back from France. "Pray, cease wasting time!" Lady Honoria snapped. "We need wine from the cellar and… Where is Adam? I gave him plain instruction to place a bouquet in each window! Our guests are due in but one hour!"

As she disappeared into the hallway, Sir Miles sighed.

The feast successfully concluded, the long tables were pushed aside to make way for the dancing. As the musicians tuned their *instruments, the guests stood in clusters, murmuring to one another. Noblemen from neighbouring estates mingled with royal courtiers, naval officials with ambassadors, a sea of jewels, rich fabrics and shimmering embroidery. The scent of perfumes mingled with the lingering traces of roast meats and the sweaty odour of over-dressed old men.*

Ladies of the local gentry, resplendent in their gowns, took their seats along the walls, fans in hand, appraising the scene. They whispered among themselves, eyeing one another's jewellery with tight, competitive smiles. Servants moved like wraiths through the room, refilling goblets, ensuring the guests were never without drink or a diversion.

Anne Standish, in her element, glanced waspishly at her sisters, Margaret and Elizabeth, standing with their husbands. Elizabeth had married the wool merchant, Edward Carter, a kindly gentleman, as rich as he was dull. After a string of ill-fated matches - and a great deal of foot-stamping - Margaret had been ordered by her father to wed Archibald, Duke of Montrose.

Anne smiled to herself. Montrose! She had never heard of the place and had to be informed that it was in the Highlands of Scotland, among the thistles and brambles of that godforsaken realm. The Duke - a perfectly humourless fellow with bright orange hair - had insisted, they move there.

And there Margaret languished, lady of all Montrose.

Peering into the far corner of the hall, Anne spotted Jacob, sitting by himself, cradling a silver goblet. He looked dishevelled and miserable.

Striding across the room, she pulled him to his feet. "Your face is spoiling my party," she told him.

Draining the goblet, he looked down at her, smiling apologetically.

"And you're drunk," she said flatly.

"All these… puffed-up nobles," he said, gesturing around the room. "'Tis too much to bear, sister. If I am indeed spoiling your party, then perhaps 'tis best if I take my leave?"

Anne's glare softened. "Nay, Jacob. I hear Father has plans for you, and you must not disappoint him."

Jacob groaned. Disappointing Sir Miles seemed to his specialty.

Anne plucked a stray piece of candied orange from Jacob's periwig, flicking it toward a portrait of Lady Honoria, where it clung absurdly to their mother's painted décolletage.

The pair giggled. "Come," said Anne. "I shall introduce you to the Duke of Loxley. He's incorrigible."

Jacob groaned once again.

Sir Miles paced to the centre of the dance floor. "My Lords, ladies and gentlemen, pray silence!" he bellowed, and waited patiently for a hush to descend. "I have an announcement to make."

"Boring!" came the heckle, in a voice Jacob now recognised as Loxley's.

Sir Miles ignored the interruption, as the ladies gathered around the unsteady duke muttered their rebukes. Jacob, meanwhile, suddenly felt very sober.

Reaching into his pocket, Sir Miles pulled out a chunky gold ring and held it aloft for all to see. "My youngest son, Jacob, is now heir to the Standish name," he announced. "This ring, which I hold before you, was gifted to my grandfather, Edward Standish, by His Majesty, King Charles I, as a token of his loyalty and service. It has passed through our family, and now it is Jacob's to wear, in honour of those who have come before him."

His vivid blue eyes sought out Jacob, who was standing awkwardly at the edge of the room. "Step forward, Jacob," he said.

Reluctantly, Jacob approached, his discomfort palpable.

Sir Miles held out the ring. "Wear it with honour, my son."

Jacob hesitated for a moment before accepting the ring, sliding it onto his index finger. When he realised with horror that it was too wide, he swapped it onto his middle finger. Still it was loose.

Steadying it with a thumb, he self-consciously inspected the design: the Standish family crest, rendered expertly in enamel. Never had he witnessed such workmanship, and it only added to his sense of futility.

A hush and fallen over the room, as though everyone expected of him some eloquent acceptance speech, but Jacob could find no words.

Loxley's voice rang out again. "Try not to lose it!"

A ripple of laughter spread through the guests; only Jacob and Sir Miles appeared stony-faced.

Afterwards, Jacob was engulfed in a throng, obliged to extend his hand for all to see. Some pawed at the ring while others demanded to wear it; Jacob refused, conscious of its value and significance. Already, he was petrified of losing such a precious heirloom.

As the gawpers drifted away, Anne sidled up to him. "You know 'tis cursed?"

"I beg your pardon?" He studied her face for the hint of a grin, but there was none.

"Father's grandfather, Edward, was slain by an arrow shot by one of his own soldiers, as he showed the ring to another," she said.

Jacob reached for a nearby goblet. "'Tis pure coincidence."

Anne's eyes gleamed. "They say the soldier swore he saw the ring's enamel shimmer ere he loosed the arrow - as if it had beckoned the shot."

"What nonsense!" Jacob exclaimed, though he did not sound convinced.

"Edward's son, Simon - our grandfather - swore to never wear the ring, deeming it cursed. Yet one stormy night, when he

was full of wine, he took it from its hiding place and placed it on his finger, swearing he would break the Standish superstition once and for all. He wore it to bed, and the following morning was found dead, the ring still on his finger."

"Why do you tease me so?"

"His hand had turned black, they said, as if the ring's very metal had poisoned him."

"Do not believe a word of it, Jacob." Sir Miles, unnoticed, had joined them. "I have heard the same tales. They are but frivolous nonsense," he added cheerily, slapping his son on the back and turning to the musicians. "Come, all! We must dance!" he announced, to great cheers.

Brow furrowed, Jacob stared at the ring. As Anne moved away, heading towards Loxley, the musicians' sprightly tune entered his mind.

The vibrant hues of the ladies' gowns - deep burgundies, soft greens, golds - shimmered as they spun. The music rose and fell, and the hall became a blur of colour and motion, a living tapestry of silk and brocade, gaiety and mirth, set to the rhythm of lute, harpsichord and viol.

Jacob drained the goblet. "I need more wine," he said to himself.

The next morning, he woke under a table, his head throbbing and his mouth drier than the sweepings of a hearth. As his misted mind swirled, memories darted from the fog, he started and felt, in a rising panic, for the ring.

It was gone.

Chapter Eighteen

La Morte Part II

The Great Chapel was empty save for the inquisitors, the French guards having left with the disconsolate Mr Pepys.

Abby joined Jacob at the side of the coffin. "What is it, Jacob?" she asked.

Despite herself, she brushed the back of her fingers against Sophie de Valois's cheek, so perfectly smooth it resembled porcelain. It was cold - so unnaturally cold - that she pulled back with a gasp.

Jacob was too mired in his own thoughts to notice. "The gloves," he said, pointing. "What do you notice?"

She shook her head.

"The middle finger of her right hand," he prompted.

"A lump? She's wearing a ring?"

"Aye," he said, reaching in and gently sliding the soft leather glove from Sophie's hand.

As he removed the ring, which was loose, he dropped it with a strangled moan into the coffin and stumbled backward.

Abby retrieved it, puzzled, holding it in her hand. "What is it, Jacob?"

Then she recognised the enamel design from a crest she had lately seen in his house. It was the coat of arms of the Standish family of Greenwich.

"That ring," he said, pointing with a trembling finger. "That ring was given to me by my father and stolen more than a year ago. How the blazes has it found its way onto Sophie de Valois's corpse?"

Abby stared, bewildered, at the ring.

"My sister told me it was cursed," he said.

As Abby looked on, Jacob lifted Sophie's hand and slid the ring back onto her finger.

"What are you doing, Jacob?" she asked. "That ring – 'tis yours."

"Nay," he replied, furrowed of brow, as he struggled to replace Sophie's glove on her limp hand. "I never wish to see it again."

Chapter Nineteen

Taking Stock

Back at their apartment, Abby and Jacob sat across from one another at the big table, lost in thought. Their rain-sodden clothing steamed gently on their bodies as the fire warmed them up.

"Where do we start, Jacob?"

He pulled off his hat and periwig and cast them towards the fireplace to dry. "The ring," he said, drumming his fingers on the table. "The ring."

"How was it stolen?" she asked.

After Jacob had recounted the events of that long night in May the previous year - omitting his own drunkenness - she asked, "Who were the guests at this party?"

Jacob sucked in his lower lip. "Anne would know far better than I," he said. "But there were several courtiers in attendance..." He paused, scrunching his eyes tight shut in concentration. "There was an awfully brash gentleman, who was mighty rude to me. Roxbury? Lockley?"

"Loxley?"

"Aye, that was his name. You know him?"

"He's here, Jacob, in this court."

Jacob's mouth fell open. "Was it he who stole my ring and placed it upon poor Sophie's hand?"

"Who else was present at the party? Arabella Wyndham? Molly Tanner? Hakewill?"

Clutching the sides of his head, Jacob moaned. "I do not remember, Abby. We shall have to ask my sister."

Abby raised an eyebrow. "Is that so?" she said. "Your powers of observation are usually more acute, Jacob."

"I confess, my recollections of that night are fogged by wine."

She sighed deeply.

"What troubles you?" he asked.

"We're trapped here, aren't we, Jacob? In this place where we don't belong."

"The King himself requested your presence."

"Aye, and Mr Pepys dressed me in his wife's clothing. I feel like a rag doll trussed up in finery."

He reached across to take her hand, and discovered the table was too wide.

As he pulled it back, she laughed. "At least you're here with me, Jacob. I'd be lost without you."

They went on to discuss the facts of the case. Somebody – the murderer – had positioned Sophie beneath the sabotaged chandelier by moving the French chair, fully aware that she would sit there. It had to be a court insider, someone who knew her well.

Then there was the note, discovered secreted within the hem of her cuff. It was the reason Sophie had been in the Vane Room at midnight, waiting - or so she thought - for Mr Pepys.

Jacob thumped the table angrily. "'Twas not he who murdered Mistress de Valois!"

"Never, Jacob, I know him too well - he would never do such a thing. He's been framed by whoever possessed that note and handed it to Sophie to contrive her demise."

"Who could that be?"

Abby shrugged.

"And the tear in the paper?" he asked.

"Perhaps a simple accident?"

A distant bell chimed the second hour, causing Jacob's stomach to rumble.

"You copied the text," he said. "Show it to me."

Light steps could be heard descending the stairs, and the servant girl, Betsy appeared. She took one look at the bedraggled inquisitors and gasped, "Oh my! You should have called me, mistress - and good sir! Pray, forgive me. I shall find you fresh attire." As she scampered back upstairs, she called back, "Dinner will arrive presently!"

Shortly, Abby and Jacob were dressed in dry clothing, seated before a veritable feast of a dozen roasted quail glazed with honey, spiced apples and a crusty pie filled with venison, chestnuts and wild herbs. Bowls of bread and butter sat among platters of roasted vegetables, while a jug of mulled cider steamed invitingly between them, giving off a wonderful odour of cinnamon and cloves.

"I could become accustomed to this," Jacob enthused through a mouthful.

Abby's copied note was on the table between them and had already become stained with butter. Jacob pulled it towards him with the little finger of a hand clutching a quail.

She had penned the words as she recalled them.

> *Sir*
> *Deliver th*
> *the utmost dis*
> *lady I did mentio*
> *await me at midnig*
> *Vane Room.*
> *Trust none but her.*
> *Yours in confidence*
> *Samuel Pepys*

"What are the missing words?" he asked.

"Here, hand it back," she said.

Jacob pushed it across the table as she pulled out her ink and quill. As he continued to gorge, she bent over the page, scribbling intently. At last, she pushed it back toward him.

> *Sir*
> *Deliver th is note with*
> *the utmost dis cretion to the*
> *lady I did mentio n who must*
> *await me at midnig ht in the*
> *Vane Room.*
> *Trust none but her.*
> *Yours in confidence*
> *Samuel Pepys*

Jacob read it and nodded. "It does make sense. I wonder to whom it was addressed, to pass on to Mistress de Valois?"

"A gentleman," was all she could offer. "If only we could speak with Mr Pepys. We must discover where he's held. And get word to His Majesty."

"Indeed. I believe you are best placed for the task."

Sighing, she nodded. "We should consider our list of suspects. Who would wish Sophie dead?"

Jacob picked his teeth with a small bone from his plate. "Hakewill, for one. He knows of her spying and loathes the profligacy of His Majesty's mistresses."

"Did he attend Anne's party? Might he have stolen your ring?"

Jacob shook his head apologetically. "We must ask my sister."

"I'll make a list," said Abby, retrieving paper from her bag and writing:

Hakewill

"Who else?" she asked. "Loxley's a suspect, given he may have stolen your ring at the party, and was betrothed to Sophie ere the King stole her from him."

Loxley

Glancing towards the door and then the stairs, to check no one could overhear, he whispered, "Dare we mention the King himself?"

"Jacob!" she said, then caught herself. "We dare not utter his name in connection with this crime," she murmured. "And I'll not commit it to paper."

"Yet he knew of her spying, which might have sparked a war betwixt our nations."

Abby quickly changed the subject. "What of the mistresses?"

"It goes without saying. Their jealousy is rife."

Abby wrote their names.

Arabella Wyndham
Molly Tanner
Isabel March

Her quill hovered over the paper after she had finished, and Jacob noticed she was avoiding his gaze.

Then suddenly his sunken cheeks flushed red, and his jaw tightened. "Nay," he said menacingly.

She sucked in a breath. "We're inquisitors, Jacob. 'Tis our duty to be thorough."

He rose in an instant, towering over the table and sending his chair toppling backwards. "I will hear no more of it. My beloved sister is no murderer, of that I can assure you. If you pen her name there, I will…" He stopped, lost for words.

Abby sat back, eyes pleading. "I would never betray you or your family, Jacob, but we have a duty to Mr Pepys and to the King."

"Never!" he roared, angrier than she had ever seen him, and fled the house, the slamming of the heavy oak door reverberating around the room.

Abby wiped her forehead with a sleeve.

With a heavy heart, she wrote at the bottom of the list:

Anne Standish

It had to be done.

Chapter Twenty

Piles of Gold

Abby was still staring at the suspect list when a knock came on the door. So distracted was she that she rose to answer it, slipping into her old maid's routine. Only as she stood, did she remember who she was now: no longer the servant, but the mistress of the house.

Play your part, she thought, *and play it well, Abigail.*

Sitting back down, she smoothed her red robe at the thighs. "Enter!"

A palace messenger appeared in the doorway, the King's crest on his doublet. "Mistress Harcourt, your company is requested at Mistress Wyndham's residence."

Instinctively, she glanced around for Jacob and let out a shuddering sigh.

The messenger tilted his head. "Mistress?"

"'Tis nought," she said, swatting an imaginary fly. "Where is Mistress Wyndham's residence? I know it not."

The messenger bowed. "I have been instructed to escort the mistress," he said.

With a start, she remembered Mr Pepys and his dire predicament. "But first, I wish to see the King – as a matter of some urgency."

"I believe that His Majesty is presently with Mistress Wyndham, mistress. They are playing cards."

The day's storm having run its course, the drenched streets and alleyways shimmered as the messenger led Abby between the ornamental lawns of the Privy Garden. Many of the pathways were in a dilapidated state, and she took care to step over puddles, some of which appeared disconcertingly deep.

The marble-and-bronze statues amid each of the square lawns depicted classical figures. Abby recognised Apollo, playing his lyre; and there, Diana the huntress, with bow in hand; behind her, Mercury, captured mid-flight on winged sandals.

The wet grass smelled fresh and life-affirming, and, for a fleeting moment, her cares drifted away.

Led to the south-west corner of the garden, in the shadow of a row of tall elm trees, Abby emerged into a wide street lined with austere Tudor-style buildings. In the distance, to her right, was the Holbein Gate, and, looming above her, a similarly imposing twin-towered gate, with a large central passage for coach access and twin archways on either side for pedestrians.

"The King Street Gate," said the messenger, sensing Abby's curiosity. "Mistress Wyndham's residence is through this arch," he added, gesturing for her to follow.

Arabella's house on King Street, though Tudor in origin, now exuded Restoration elegance. The timbered frontage had been mostly concealed beneath a fresh facade of pale stone, giving it a refined appearance that spoke to the lady's wealth and ambitions. Above the entryway, a small balcony jutted out, framed by wrought-iron railings, from which to survey the bustling street below - and from which to be seen.

The door itself was painted a deep, glossy green and bore a brass knocker shaped like a lion's head. Either side of the entrance, stone urns brimming with ivy sat atop squat pillars. Many of the materials and adornments looked new, as if the carpenters and stonemasons had been called back again and again, to add little touches for an owner intent upon perfection.

A youthful manservant wearing a silver-buttoned coat answered the door. Having introduced Abby, the messenger took his leave. She was ushered into a long hallway with soaring, Tudor-style arches that had been overlaid with elaborate plasterwork, each arch carved with swirling leaves and delicate rosettes picked out in gold.

Towards the end of the hallway, the servant opened a door. "The Drawing Room, Mistress Harcourt," he intoned.

It was unlike any withdrawing room she had visited before.

The walls were lined with tapestries ten feet high and vast paintings in gilded frames - classical and biblical scenes, and portraits of Arabella Wyndham herself, resplendent in silks, smiling demurely - and the high leaded windows were draped with floral-patterned damask.

There were tables of solid silver and cabinets imported from Japan, displaying ornaments crafted in gold. A group of musicians, off to one corner, played while the occupants of the room caroused. Couples on sofas lounged across one another, the ladies displaying enough flesh to make Cromwell moan in his grave, while servants filled goblets with wine.

Amid all this was a grand oak table, at one end of which were seated four people whom Abby recognised instantly: Mistresses Wyndham and Tanner, the Duke of Loxley, and His Majesty the King.

Each held a hand of playing cards, besides Molly Tanner, who was nibbling Loxley's ear. In front of each was a pile of glinting gold guineas, each coin worth half a year's wages for a maidservant, with the size of their gains varying widely.

The King's pile, sprawling so haphazardly that several coins had spilled to the floor, was by far the largest, and Abby guessed it must hold at least a couple of thousand guineas. Mistress Wyndham's was the most paltry – Abby counted just seven coins.

As the servant stepped forward to introduce the new arrival, Molly, glimpsing Abby from behind Loxley's periwig, broke off from her flirting, and waved excitedly. "Abigail!" she called out. "Come and join us!"

Loxley groaned exaggeratedly and slapped Molly's thigh. "Must she really? She is so frightfully poor!"

As he leaned in to kiss Molly on the cheek, she pushed him away and he slipped from his chair, arms flailing, to the raucous delight of his companions. Loxley was clearly very drunk – as were they.

So these are the 'veritable agents of sin', of whom Hakewill spoke, Abby thought, rooted to the spot.

While she had served inebriated guests at certain of Mr Pepys's late-night parties, the worst behaviour she had endured involved a bout of intolerably tuneless lute-playing. *This* resembled a scene from the dark hellscapes rendered by Hieronymous Bosch and made her feel like an innocent child.

The King beckoned Abby over. He was wearing a rich, brocaded amber doublet that had fallen open to reveal a wine-stained shirt. "Play some Primero with us, Abigail Harcourt," he said, slurring a little. "'Tis a most enchanting game - though hardly as enchanting as you." His lopsided grin revealed teeth the colour of driftwood.

Loxley, who had by now found his feet, gave Charles a shove to the chest. "Hands off!" he said, also slurring. "She's mine!"

Abby was saved by Molly, who rose from the table and took her by the arm. "On the contrary, gents," she told them in a lilting voice, "Abigail Harcourt is mine!" With that, she led the inquisitor towards a sofa beneath one of the windows, while Loxley cat-called after them.

"But... I need to speak with His Majesty," Abby protested as she was dragged away.

"Let the boys calm themselves, sweetheart. First, we gossip," Molly replied with a grin.

In the glow of the many dozens of candles placed around the room, Molly looked more dazzling than ever. Her blue eyes glinted like sapphires, set within her heart-shaped face, and her long, curly auburn hair, untied and free, lay splayed across her shoulders. Dressed in silk that matched her eyes, she made Abby feel self-consciously plain.

"Where are Isabel March and Anne Standish?" the inquisitor asked, since the King's other mistresses seemed to be missing out on the entertainment.

"Isabel and her husband have fled to Spain," Molly replied, "ere he loses his head. Anne, I heard tell, is away hunting."

Familiar with Molly's loose tongue, Abby asked brazenly, "Who do you think murdered Sophie de Valois?"

Molly, swigging from her goblet, froze with a look of pure shock. "*Sophie is dead?*"

"You were not told?"

Molly's right cheek twitched, she snorted, then, unable to control herself, laughed so hard that her mouthful of red wine sprayed across the expensive floor. Nudging Abby playfully, she said with a smile, "I'm rather good, aren't I! At acting, I mean."

The inquisitor's expression remained blank.

Molly continued, "Aye, word of her death spread like… well, Mistress de Valois's reputation!" Cue another bout of hysterics, before she leaned in to add *sotto voce*, "I heard it was the Catholics."

"Is Sophie not a Catholic herself?"

"Secretly, aye, 'tis said. And French Catholics murdered her for consorting with an Anglican king."

Abby scratched her cheek thoughtfully. Religion was another angle entirely, and one the inquisitors had not considered.

"I heard there were celebrations in the streets once word reached the people, and that fights broke out 'twixt the English and the French Huguenots," Molly went on. "Charlie told me…"

Her attention was drawn to a commotion breaking out at the King's card table. Loxley's monkey, Figaro, appeared to have swiped one of His Majesty's coins, and the King was now chasing the creature around the room, cursing loudly, yet spluttering with delight. "Return to me my guinea, Mr Figaro, you beastly parasite!" he chided, stumbling and rising, as the squealing monkey swung from a chandelier, "Or I shall have your tiny head!"

The assembled courtiers hooted with merriment at the scene, and at their King's fine way with words. Abby had never witnessed anything like it.

She outlined the story of Mr Pepys's incarceration to Molly, who informed her that he was likely held in the Porter's Lodge, which had seen use as a makeshift jail. It relieved Abby, who was concerned he might have been dragged to the Tower - a grim fate that no man warranted - and she resolved to visit him at the earliest opportunity.

"I'm worried also about Jacob," she said.

Molly squinted, puzzled. "Jacob?"

"My fellow inquisitor."

The King's young mistress beamed. "The tall fellow! The one who wears such outdated garb!"

Outdated? Abby thought. It had never crossed her mind; being fashionable was something she could ill afford, let alone concern herself with. Merely clothing herself against the elements was the best she could hope for.

"Have you seen the size of his shoe-buckles?" Molly continued, stifling her glee with a hand. "They're so large!"

Abby smiled to humour her. She liked the young woman and greatly appreciated her camaraderie, but she also had better things to do than gossip about shoe buckles. "I must speak with the King," she said, rising impatiently.

"Mistress Harcourt!" Charles greeted her, as she approached.

Abby bowed, and he held out his hand for her to kiss.

"Pray, do not forget me!" Loxley quipped, extending his own hand, which the King batted aside, chuckling.

Arabella sat stock still, cards in hand, three gold guineas on the table before her, staring icily at Abby, swaying slightly in her seat. She mouthed something to her; Abby read it as "I have your measure," and ignored it.

"I need more coins, Charles," she told the King, pursing her wine-stained lips provocatively, "lest I can play no longer."

"Then you must leave the game, Arabella," he replied, eyes fixed on his cards.

"Lend her another ten thousand, you miserly rogue!" said Loxley. "Or at least give the old crone another castle to sell!"

As Charles rounded on the Duke, Arabella shot to her feet, teeth bared like a cornered fox. Her billowing silk gown knocked over her goblet, spilling wine across the table, soaking the cards already played and running through the stacked coins.

The two men leapt up to avoid the ruby-red liquid that was spilling over the table's edge.

Abby could only stare anxiously at the scene, wishing the floor would swallow her whole.

Arabella's face contorted with rage as she snatched up the toppled goblet and hurled it at the King, missing by a wide margin, to Loxley's great amusement. "I will play more Primero!" she shrieked, all semblance of control abandoned.

The King moved swiftly around the table and gave her a firm push toward the door. "Guards!" he called. "Escort this bitter old harridan from the room! She shames herself - and her King!"

As the guards stationed at the door rushed forward, Arabella planted her feet and clutched fistfuls of the King's shirt, her face twisted with fury. "You've seen nought yet, Charlie boy," she snarled.

Each guard took one of her arms and marched Arabella backwards from the room, heels stuttering across the flagstones, her menacing gaze never diverted from the King.

Without warning, Molly rose from her sofa and began performing a Tyburn jig, pointedly eyeing her departing rival. Her kicks grew more spasmodic until, with a flourish, she threw herself to the ground and played dead. The room erupted in laughter and applause.

"You won't last, whore!" Arabella yelled, as the door slammed behind her.

"More wine!" cried the King.

As normality - or what passed for it - was restored, the King bade Abby take Mistress Wyndham's vacated seat.

Desperate to help her employer, she came straight to the point. "Your Majesty, I beg you to free Mr Pepys from his cruel incarceration. You know him, Sire - he'd never commit murder. He is innocent."

The King arched an eyebrow. "Say you."

Abby's freckled cheek twitched. "*Say I*, Your Majesty?"

Slapping his exquisitely garbed knee, he tutted jovially. "Let us drop this dreadful formality, Abigail. You must address me as Charles."

She shook her head. "I could never do that, Your Majesty. It would not... sit well with me. You are my King, after all."

"As you prefer, I wish only that you are comfortable at my court." He paused. "As to the matter of Mr Pepys, how can you be certain that he is innocent?"

"Since murder does not befit him."

The King glanced toward Loxley and reached out to clasp his shoulder. "The Duke here, I have known since we were boys – have I not, James?"

Loxley grinned back. "And he has grown in stature, if not in wisdom."

Removing his hand, the King returned his gaze to Abigail. "But friendship has its bounds where foreign politics are concerned, my dear. My hands are tied. The French believe the note implicates Pepys, and I cannot be seen to overrule them. By the same token, I could not release Loxley simply because I do not believe him capable of a crime. You must prove Pepys's innocence." He leaned closer. "Can you do that?"

Wordlessly, she wrung her hands.

"You do seem rather… young," he added, smiling affectedly, "for the role of inquisitor."

Loxley spluttered, slapped the King's back heartily, and the pair of them dissolved into giggles.

Abby could only look on, feeling smaller and less worthy than ever.

"Tell her who did it, Charles," said Loxley, still chuckling. "Nothing takes place in Whitehall without the

King's knowledge. Did you have her murdered, perchance, Charlie boy?"

The King's expression hardened, and he stared at Loxley, his upper lip curled in disdain. "Know your boundaries, James. My patience is not without its limits." He turned to Abby. "'Tis upon you, inquisitor, to discover who murdered my beloved Sophie. And once their name is known to me, then mark my words, they shall answer for their despicable crime."

It was a reminder to her of the King's awful power over life and death. He had shown her nothing but politeness, yet was capable of the darkest decisions, as so many of his opponents had discovered to their cost. This was not an investigation she could mishandle - lives were at stake. Her own included, should she make a catastrophic blunder.

"Whom do you believe murdered my Sophie?" the King asked.

The question caught Abby off guard, and she blurted out, "There is no love lost 'twixt your mistresses, Your Majesty."

Charles narrowed his eyes. "You consider one of my dearest loves capable of such devilry?"

"Well... I..."

"What absolute nonsense!" the King spluttered, nudging Loxley, and the two men recommenced their hysterics.

Chapter Twenty-One

The Walls Have Ears

Abby was relieved to slip away from the Drawing Room unnoticed, as the royal party resumed their card game, goblets freshly filled. The decadence and debauchery had upset her. *How much wealth is won and lost on the turn of a card?* she wondered. *The King's court has grown wild. Little wonder there are murmurings of dissent in the city.*

How dearly she missed Jacob's steadying influence – his charming naivety, his loyalty, his strength. She resolved to return to their lodgings, where she hoped to find him and reconcile their differences. If it meant striking Anne Standish's name from their list of suspects, then so be it. She had not expected to feel so adrift without him.

Abby was acutely aware of the urgency in tracking down Mr Pepys at the Porter's Lodge. The poor man, unaccustomed as he was to the indignities of incarceration, was still less deserving of such a fate.

She dearly wished she could offer him a glimmer of hope - she was his appointed inquisitor, after all; it was her responsibility to extricate him from his predicament. Yet the King had denied her pleas to secure his release.

What could she possibly offer the poor man, besides hollow reassurances?

If only she could uncover some crucial breakthrough before facing the dear Pepys.

Arabella's soaring hallway was empty as she headed for the exit, marvelling at the riches the woman had accumulated: a rare timepiece, an Italian marble bust, a painting by Rembrandt. She flaunted her influence over the King without shame.

But is that influence waning? wondered Abby. Arabella had been the King's favoured mistress for many years; these days, his affections appeared to have shifted.

As Abby passed one door, she caught the voice of a teenage boy from behind it, raised and insistent. "When will he act, Mother? I tire of your excuses."

Stopping, she cupped an ear to the wooden door panel. The reply came in Arabella's voice. "I have tried often, but Charles acts as and when he wishes! My hands are tied."

"Then untie them! Why must I wait? The Queen is barren, dull, and foreign to boot, and here am I, a just and rightful English heir…"

"Yet you are not just and rightful, Henry, since Charles and I remain unwed…"

Their voices were becoming louder, and Abby fancied she could hear the gritting of the pair's teeth. Pepys had once mentioned Arabella's son by the King, though she could not remember his name. Now she knew - it was Henry.

"When will he divorce her?" Henry railed, accompanied by a loud bang, presumably a fist on the table.

"Lower your voice!" Arabella hissed. "The walls have ears."

If only she knew, thought Abby.

But the lad was not to be quelled. "I tire of cowering in the shadows, Mother! The throne deserves strength and a legacy. How is it fair that Queen Catherine holds her title, while I am denied mine? When will I become Duke? I am the King's son, for Heaven's sake!"

"His bastard son, Henry."

"Then my father must divorce and take you as his wife!"

"The people will not allow it!" Arabella was becoming animated also, the wine loosening her tongue.

"Then wed the King in secret! The people need not know."

"I deserve to be Queen."

"Aye, Mother, and your craven delays threaten our position. My father is fickle, his attentions turn to the latest mistress like a weathervane in the wind."

"Can you not see that timing is everything? Press him too hard and he retreats."

"And while you tarry, others gain his ear. Are we to lose our grip for the sake of your caution?"

"Do not mistake impatience for strength!"

"Nor hesitation for wisdom!"

The room fell silent. "Is not Sophie dead?" Arabella purred.

Abby raised a hand to her mouth, and in doing so accidentally rapped a knuckle on the door.

"What was that?" Henry asked sharply.

A deathly hush descended, as those inside strained their ears for further sounds.

"Check the door!" Arabella hissed.

By the time he had opened it, and scanned the hallway, Abby was nowhere to be seen.

Chapter Twenty-Two

All Time Low

Abby's mind raced as she retraced the steps to her lodgings. A watery sun threatened to pierce the clouds, mirroring the investigation's elusive answers. So many theories, so few conclusions. Arabella had practically gloated over Mistress de Valois's death - *might she have had a hand in it?*

How she longed for Jacob's opinion. Previously, in Brampton, at the Deptford dockyard, and in the coffee houses off The Strand, she had been in the ascendancy. Her theories and deductions, her interrogations, had so often led to their success. Jacob's clumsiness had sometimes irked her, but she hid it, knowing his confidence was fragile.

Yet here, in a royal palace, she felt overwhelmed, could not see the wood for the trees.

These are merely people, albeit garbed in finery and with titles to their names, she thought. *Why am I allowing them to make me so fearful?*

The weight of the responsibility, the oppressive atmos-
phere of abused power, the pervasive claustrophobia of
the sprawling palace… It was proving all too much to
bear for her alone.

"Jacob!" she called, opening the door to find him
hunched over the table at their apartment, a tankard
clutched in his right fist.

As she ran towards him, he looked up, his hazel eyes
dulled and hooded. The indifference of his expression
stopped her in her tracks. She pulled up the chair opposite
and sat. A crackling fire was going in the hearth; its aroma
smelled of home.

When she smiled, he did not return the gesture.

Reaching out across the table, she asked gently, "What
troubles you?"

He did not react.

With a sudden jolt, Abby realised the table had been
cleared. It must have shown in her face, since Jacob's
expression changed to puzzlement tinged with suspicion.

The note, on which she had written the suspect list -
including Jacob's sister's name - was gone. *Did I put it in
my satchel?* she wondered. *Or did I leave it here on the table?*

If it had indeed been on the table - had Jacob read it?
Is that why he's acting so oddly? she wondered.

Why did I even pen Anne Standish's name there, she asked
herself, *when there really was no need?*

Opposite her, Jacob downed a healthy slug of ale and wiped his lips with the back of his hand.

"I don't believe your sister murdered Mistress de Valois," she said.

Wordlessly, he arched a thick eyebrow.

"Although I don't know her," she went on, "I do know you, Jacob, and if she is cut from the same cloth, then she would not have murder in her."

He let out a single, ironic laugh. "Why would you consider she be like me?" His speech was sluggish, and she realised with dismay that he had drunk too much wine. *Can nobody in this palace remain sober?* she thought. *What a desperate place.*

At least, she realised, *it may explain his sombre mood.*

Draining his ale, Jacob hollered out for more. The inquisitors heard footsteps begin descending the staircase.

"What if she did murder the lady?" Jacob asked, leaning his sneering face towards hers.

Abby could only shake her head solemnly.

"There was no love lost betwixt her and Sophie," he added.

"Nay, Jacob. Your own flesh and blood."

The servant, Betsy, arrived carrying a jug of ale. As she began decanting some into Jacob's tankard, Abby said, "There was a note here, on this table, bearing names...?"

"Aye, mistress."

"What became of it?"

"Why, I… I threw it in the fire, mistress." Betsy stopped pouring. Jacob snatched the jug from her and continue the refilling. "Did I do wrong?" she asked. Her coif was sitting askew on her head, and one of her fingernails was broken and bloodied.

If the note is destroyed, she realised with some relief, *Jacob can't have read it.*

"Would this be the same note in which you penned my sister's name?" Jacob asked. "As a suspect in our investigation."

"You read it?" Abby asked, barely above a whisper.

"May I be excused?" Betsy asked.

Overwhelmed with emotion, Abby snapped, "Aye!" Then fixing the servant with a glare, she added, "Begone!"

Upset, the young girl fled toward the stairs.

Downing his ale in one long swig, his Adam's apple bobbing as the frothy liquid cascaded down his neck, Jacob finished with an exaggerated gasp. "It seems you do believe my own flesh and blood capable of murder," he said, centring his periwig and donning his plumed hat.

"Nay, Jacob," she replied desperately, rounding the table towards him.

Pushing her away, he made for the door. "Stand aside," he growled, tripping over his own feet and falling flat on his face.

As he picked himself up, she handed him his hat, flinch-
ing under the weight of his anger.

"God keep you, then, Abigail Harcourt," he said, and
was gone.

Abby sank to the floor and wept.

She did not notice Betsy, standing at the foot of the
stairs, watching her.

Chapter Twenty-Three

Return of the Ring

Abby took a lonely supper that night, during which she apologised to the servant for her outburst, and it was graciously accepted. She dearly hoped that Jacob would return, bounding on long legs like that camel she had seen, replenished of good cheer and sense. But he did not. She heard footsteps outside, but all seemed bound for the Queen's maids' lodging house nearby.

What will become of us? she wondered.

If their great adventure were truly over, what would she do? Already, it meant everything to her.

Rich men, powerful men, had taken her seriously (even if the powerful women of the court were yet to be won over). Working as Mr Pepys's inquisitor had given her the opportunity to prove her worth. The long hours spent in his library had been justified – she had made something of herself.

And now, it all looked like being snatched away.

"Where are you, Jacob?" she wailed to the rafters.

As night descended, Betsy lit all the candles in the house. As she did so, the two of them fell into an easy conversation, brought on by their shared backgrounds. Outside, the rain held off, replaced by a howling wind that rattled damaged timberwork and whistled through tight spaces.

The young servant's tale went like this…

Betsy Underwood had grown up in a small village in Essex, with her father, a humble blacksmith, and her mother, who took in mending work to help make ends meet. Her father was well-liked but dangerously outspoken.

When a traveling noble's horse threw a shoe and Betsy's father refused to serve him until he paid an outstanding debt, tensions flared. The noble, insulted by the blacksmith's defiance, falsely accused him of theft. Her father was imprisoned on trumped-up charges, and, after months in a freezing cold, disease-ridden cell, he died before his trial could take place, leaving Betsy and her mother devastated and penniless.

"My own father suffered the same fate," Abby told her quietly.

Without her father's support, Betsy went on, her family had been forced from their home. Her mother found work where she could, but her health deteriorated quickly under the strain. At thirteen, Betsy was sent to live with an aunt in London, a seamstress who took her on as an apprentice. Betsy toiled tirelessly for her aunt, stitching day and night.

One day, a lady courtier commissioned a piece from her aunt's shop and noticed Betsy's skilful stitching and quiet efficiency. Impressed, she offered Betsy a position at the palace, where reliable young attendants were always in demand. It was an opportunity she could not turn down.

And here Abby found her, in luxurious surroundings, sleeping on a makeshift bed in the attic.

"You were angered by me when we first met," the inquisitor pointed out.

"And I beg your forgiveness for my insolence, mistress. I allowed my emotions to get the better of me."

Abby cupped a hand over Betsy's. "There's no need. I understand. I might well have done the same."

Betsy studied her expression, puzzled. "Yet you are the King's mistress?"

Abby snorted. "Nay, Betsy. He desires my company, that is all, and I cannot deny him."

Abruptly, the servant changed the subject. "I saw Jacob push you aside," she said.

You don't miss much, do you? Abby thought. *You'd make a fine inquisitor.* "Jacob is a good friend and the kindest of gentlemen. Pray, don't think ill of him. We share the same pressures here."

"What pressures, mistress?"

Shaking her head with a wry smile, Abby stood. "I'm going for a walk," she said. "I shan't be long."

She needed air, to clear her mind.

Knowing that much of the Whitehall Palace grounds was still unfamiliar to her, Abby retraced the route Pepys had shown them, heading toward the Privy Garden. The wind was so fierce it untied her flame-red hair, whipping it haphazardly about her face. She did not mind; battling the elements felt invigorating, and the open space like freedom.

A church bell rang in the distance, and she counted the chimes; it was midnight. Tomorrow, at the earliest opportunity, she would visit Mr Pepys in his cell, though she did not relish passing on the King's ill tidings.

It was up to her, and her alone it seemed, to solve the mystery of Sophie de Valois's murder. She pulled her cloak tight around herself as the wind cut through its fabric. The oil lamps surrounding the garden's perimeter flickered wildly in their glass casings, and she saw light within the windows of Hakewill's apartment.

As she reached the marble plinth of a statue of Apollo, a laurel wreath crowning his chiselled features, she was certain she heard a woman's cry rise above the wind's howl, followed by an ominous crash. The sounds came, she discerned, from somewhere along the route she had just walked.

Hitching up her petticoats, she hurried in that direction.

As Abby turned into the alley off Pebble Court, she froze at the sight before her.

A thick, iron-studded oaken door had toppled, pinning somebody beneath its weight, illuminated by a glow spilling from the room beyond the open doorway. A single pale hand protruded from beneath the door, clutched by King Charles himself, his shoulders trembling as he quietly whimpered.

It was the door, Abby knew, to Anne Standish's house. *Oh, Jacob*, she thought. *Let it not be her.*

Alerted to the inquisitor's approach by the clacking of her hard leather heels on stone, the King leapt to his feet. "Who is it?" he asked, his voice devoid of its usual might, peering into the darkness.

"'Tis I, Your Majesty," said Abby, arriving at the scene. "Abigail Harcourt."

He wrapped her in his embrace. "Such happenstance," he declared, almost breathless, "that Pepys's own inquisitor is witness to this tragic scene." Pausing, he let out a sob. "You must help me avenge my sweetheart."

Abby stood there awkwardly, hands at her side, incapable of returning the embrace. "What happened, Sire?" she asked. "Which poor wretch lies beneath that door?"

Kneeling, he once again took the hand that lay palm-upwards in the dirt of the street and, head bowed, let out an anguished sigh. "Oh my love, Anne," he groaned. "How did this happen?"

Abby's stomach lurched, and she dropped to her knees beside the King. "What will become of Jacob when he hears this terrible news?" she asked aloud, voice trembling.

As she spoke the words, a flicker of movement in the shadows beyond Molly Tanner's lodgings caught her eye. What appeared, on first glance, to be a large pile of old rags, was nothing of the sort. It was the huddled, dishevelled figure of a man.

"Who spoke my name?" the figure groaned.

"Jacob!" Abby gasped.

My name again, he thought, struggling for lucidity. The heap of rags stirred and grew taller as Jacob rose unsteadily, rubbing his eyes. "Abby?" he called out huskily.

Panicked, she glanced down at the King, who was eyeing her furiously, tightly shaking his head. *Indeed*, she realised, *he mustn't be allowed to witness this terrible scene.* "Stay away!" she called out.

Jacob found himself still clutching the tankard of ale that had led to his collapse in a stranger's doorway sometime after nightfall. Grimacing, he tossed it aside. *Stay away from what?* he wondered, his feet already propelling him into the street.

As his clouded mind awakened, he saw Abby some two dozen yards away, standing, hands clutched to her face. At her feet was a crouching man wearing elaborate garb. Both were illuminated by light from a doorway… An open doorway. Yet something was amiss, he was aware - terribly amiss.

Jacob stumbled forward. Abby ran to meet him, wrapping her arms around his midriff and clutching tightly. "Nay, Jacob, turn around," she urged.

Abby was distressed; instinctively, he put an arm around her, but his eyes remained fixed ahead. The door was not where it should have been - it lay on the ground, torn from its hinges. And the crouching man - that was the King himself, holding the hand of somebody trapped beneath the fallen door.

All at once, it struck him. "My sister's house!" he wailed.

With a shove, he pushed Abby aside, sending her sprawling into the mud, and broke into a run.

The King, who had been intently downcast, turned to face him, torment and anger contorting his features. "Hold there, Standish!" he commanded, rising to his feet.

But Jacob did not hold there. He continued running and bowled headlong into His Majesty, unable to quell his momentum. He had not intended to send them both crumpling to the ground, nor to hear the King's head strike the paving with a sickening thud. He was only dimly aware of Abby's scream as it happened.

Quick, heavy footsteps echoed from around the corner, and two armed royal guards appeared.

Charles sat up, rubbing the back of his head, dazed. Jacob, still on all fours, reacted swiftly, scrambling toward the hand protruding from beneath the door - a lifeless, upturned hand that he now knew belonged to his sister.

His breath caught as he saw the gold band shimmering dimly on her middle finger, too wide for her yet held in place between her fingers. Rising to his knees, he threw back his head, turned his palms to the heavens and let out the pitiful, guttural sound of a mortally wounded animal.

"Guards! Arrest this man!" came the King's command.

Abby flung herself at the King's feet, sobbing. "Please, Sire, I beg you - he is overwrought. Forgive him!"

Jacob managed to clasp his sister's hand, just as the guards reached him. By the time they had managed to drag him free, a sword-tip at his throat, her pale arm to the elbow had become visible.

He stared down at it in mute horror, his mouth opening and closing, unable to form words.

The King appeared in his face, those wine-stained royal lips set into a snarl. "She is mine, Jacob Standish. Not yours."

Chapter Twenty-Four

Sounds in the Darkness

Jacob said nothing - in truth, he had no words - as Abby pleaded for his life. He had struck the King, and the consequences could be unimaginable.

The more she gabbled, the less attention His Majesty paid her. As additional guards arrived, he was more intent upon securing the area. "You, guard that route," he ordered, "and you, that one. None must witness this terrible scene."

When some semblance of order was restored, the King seemed to remember Abby's presence. Taking her trembling hand in his, he said quietly, "There were riots in the streets when word of Sophie's death spread. It must not happen again. Speak no word of this to anyone."

"And Jacob?" she asked, her voice desperate.

The King turned, observing the inquisitor's hunched figure leaning against a wall, head bowed and motionless. When he faced Abby again, his features had softened. "'Tis perhaps as hard for a man to lose a sister as to lose a lover. I will pardon his recklessness," he said, pausing. "For you, Abigail."

Abby fought back tears of gratitude and relief. "Then I am forever in your debt, Your Majesty."

The King's grip on her hand tightened - painfully so. "Then discover who murdered my beloved Anne," he told her.

Jacob having been led away - to where, she dared not ask - Abby shifted her focus to the scene of the crime, acutely aware of the burden now resting squarely on her narrow shoulders.

She noticed the Standish family ring, just as Jacob had before her. How, she wondered, had it been moved from Sophie de Valois's dead hand to Anne Standish's? And who could have done so?

Turning her attention to the door, a thought crossed her mind: could Anne's death have been a tragic accident? Perhaps the aged, rusted Tudor hinges had simply given way as the door was pulled open...

Yet a cursory inspection proved her deeper fears founded. The hinges had been tampered with.

Where the heavy iron fixings should have been, only empty holes remained; the nails themselves were nowhere to be seen.

With the King distracted, busy plotting the covert removal of Anne's body, Abby skirted around the prone door and slipped into the house.

She was confronted with the same scene that her fellow inquisitor had encountered only the previous morning. *Two murders in as many days*, she thought grimly. *This devil works quickly.*

Her gaze swept the room - tapestries, a harpsichord, a table littered with gold and silver trinkets, portraits by Peter Lely… *What do I seek?* she wondered.

Shaking her head, trying to marshall her thoughts, she ascended the stairs. At the top, just as Jacob had done, she tried the first door on her left. It creaked as it opened, and Abby glanced furtively inside. *Why am I nervous of being discovered?* she wondered. *I'm an inquisitor, and this is my duty.* Yet she could not shake a sense of unease, as though she were trespassing on hallowed ground.

The only light inside the room came from the candles flickering in the corridor outside. Abby could just make out the grand four-poster bed; the rest was but murky shapes.

As she stepped inside, she swore she heard something, if very faint, like air being drawn through dry reeds. It seemed to come from near the bed.

She froze. She had heard something similar only recently. Hakewill's wheezing, she realised with a start. *Is *he in here, hiding in this room?* she wondered. Her senses heightened as her pulse quickened.

"Sir William?" she called softly into the darkness.

No reply came.

"Sir William?"

Silence.

Your imagination runs away with you, Abigail Harcourt, she chastised herself.

Then came a rustling sound near the far wall, and she let out a yelp. Steeling herself, she strode into the corridor, pulled a candle from its sconce, and shone its warm light into the room. Her eyes darted over the dressing table with its jars and trinkets, the bedside table cluttered with papers, and the studded trunk at the foot of the bed, before locking onto her quarry.

There, at the foot of the far wall: a cage filled with rodents, clambering over one another as if to escape the invasive light. *The sound must have come from there,* she thought.

Exhaling gratefully, she had just noticed the shrouded, bell-shaped object hanging from a rafter when the King's voice called sharply from downstairs. "Mistress Harcourt! Abigail!"

Gingerly, she closed the door, careful not to let it creak, and tiptoed quickly down the stairs.

"Your Majesty," she said, joining him.

"What were you doing up there?" he asked sternly.

"Investigating the mistress's murder?" Sucking in her lower lip, she realised she had phrased it like a question.

"I granted you no such leave."

Abby had no reply.

"And what did you discover?" he asked.

"Mistress Standish's door was sabotaged," she said. "The nails were removed. Whoever first opened that door was fated to be crushed."

The King covered his face with his hands. "My dear, sweet Anne. You deserved no such end."

"Where had she been, Sire?"

Eyeing the nearby guard, the King ushered Abby into a corner and spoke in a low voice. "I met with her in St James's Park earlier tonight, as she returned from hunting. We," he hesitated, "tarried there a while ere I escorted her to her lodgings."

"Was the door locked?"

He pondered for a moment. "Aye," he replied. "We would find the key in her right hand." Glancing at the door, he winced.

"And 'twas she who opened the door?" Abby asked.

Realisation dawned on the King, and he took a step backwards. "Might I have died in her place? Was it I the foul miscreant did target?"

"Nay, Sire. I feel it more likely that Mistress Standish was the target. 'Tis her apartment, the means of murder, as with Mistress de Valois, was sabotage – and she wears the Standish ring."

"What is this ring you speak of?"

"A murderer's grim signature, Sire."

The King rubbed his chin, downcast. "These heinous murders threaten to destabilise my kingdom. If my mistresses are so easily dispatched, why not I?"

Abby could only nod.

"Mistress Abigail," he continued gravely. "You came here as my guest, yet now you act as inquisitor. It stirs courtly whispers, which may leak into the city – I cannot allow it. You have but one more day to solve this devilish crime. After that, you must leave. Your presence foments suspicion."

Blinking rapidly, Abby blurted out, "But what of Mr Pepys, Your Majesty?"

"Find the true culprit, Abigail. You have twenty-four hours."

"May I visit him?"

He smiled faintly. "Indeed you may. You will find him incarcerated in the Porter's Lodge."

That much, she already knew.

Chapter Twenty-Five

Dry Swallow

Abby returned to her apartment in the early hours of the morning, relieved to find cold meats and ale left out by Betsy. The candles still burned, and embers glowed in the fireplace.

Taking a seat, she slumped forward onto the table, head on her arms, and exhaled as if expelling ghosts. The day had been like no other.

Jacob was gone - to where, only God and the King knew. The situation had taken a grim toll on the pair of them, and Abby dearly wished they had never set foot in the palace.

But she was trapped. Were it not for Mr Pepys, she might even have fled under cover of darkness.

Glancing at the food, she reached for a slice of ham and placed it in her mouth. The meat was dry and tasteless, sticking to her throat as she swallowed. With a grimace, she pushed the plate away.

She stared into the fire, its fading embers rippling through the charred logs.

She remained that way for some time.

Chapter Twenty-Six

A New Dawn

As Abby's eyes flickered open the next morning, one thought consumed her: she had but one day - this day - to conclude the investigation. Fail, and the consequences might be devastating. She could not bring herself to consider Mr Pepys's fate.

The previous night, she had gone to bed fully clothed. Uncomfortable as that might have been - in the event, she was asleep in moments - she was determined to begin the day at a canter.

The addition of poor Anne Standish to the roster of dead did aid Abby's deductions; it shed light on the murderer's motives. He - or she - must have had good reason to dispatch both Anne and Sophie.

The Frenchwoman's spying could be disregarded, as could her covert Catholicism, since Anne Standish was neither spy nor Catholic. *Whatever the reason for their tragic ends, it must be something they shared,* Abby reasoned.

Loxley, she recalled, had been cuckolded by the King when Sophie was stolen away from him. Friends since childhood – the firmest of bonds – the Duke nonetheless took great pleasure in denigrating Charles, much to the King's displeasure. But while Loxley might have slain Sophie out of spite, why then kill Anne?

The remaining mistresses? Molly Tanner… Abby could not imagine her harming a flea. The ribald young actor's only crime, it seemed, was being herself in an arena where personality was subsumed for the sake of appearance and greed.

Still, she knew, she dare not discount her.

Which left Arabella Wyndham – and, quite possibly, her son, Henry. What was it they had discussed, unaware that she had overheard? Arabella's desire to wed the King in secret, securing for her son a dukedom and for herself unimaginable power and wealth.

Burying the competition could only further that aim, and the inquisitor resolved to confront the pair of them, just as soon as she had met with Pepys.

As to Sir William Hakewill, Abby dismissed the notion that he had been lurking in Anne's chamber as fanciful. Had he indeed sabotaged her door, his next act would surely have been to vacate the scene with haste, not linger upstairs like some unguarded oaf.

Yet the question remained: since he so openly abhorred the profligacy and low morals of the King's mistresses, might he still have resorted to murder?

She would need to speak with Hakewill as well.

But first: Mr Pepys.

Abby had no glad tidings for him, but her appearance would offer him some comfort. Conversant as he was with the ways of the King's court and its intrigues, she dearly hoped he might provide a clue to unravel the mystery.

She badly needed one.

Chapter Twenty-Seven

The Porter's Lodge

It was a crisp, cloudless morning, frost glistening on the palace eaves. The sun had only recently broken the horizon, bringing with it the fragile hope of a new day.

Yesterday's storm appeared to have taken its toll. As Abby passed by Anne Standish's lodgings, she saw broken tiles scattered about the ground, although the door had already been mended. Out of curiosity, she peered in through one of the windows, but the candles had all been extinguished, offering only gloom within. *How will the King explain away her disappearance?* she wondered.

Molly had told her where to find the Porter's Lodge. Via the Court Gate, she was to cross Whitehall towards the Tilt Yard. There, to the left, was a walkway, at the end of which would be her destination.

As she passed the high stone wall enclosing the Tilt Yard, she recalled talk of its illustrious past as a Tudor jousting stadium, and more recently as an arena for bear-baiting. The King, these days, preferred a more refined entertainment, aligned with his sophisticated tastes, and was more likely to be found at the nearby Cockpit Theatre, also in the palace grounds.

Past the Tilt Yard, Abby emerged into the south-eastern edge of St James's Park, the sudden spaciousness taking her by surprise. A thin layer of mist carpeted the ground, stretching as far as the eye could see. A pair of deer, one with tall antlers, stood motionless in the haze, their ears pricked and eyes fixed on her, alerted by her presence.

To Abby's left was the Old Staircase, as Molly had described, leading toward the upper level of the Holbein Gate, then along to the Privy Gallery and eventually the Vane Room. To her right stood the Porter's Lodge.

Mr Pepys is in there, she thought, almost sensing his presence.

The lodge was a modest, timber-framed building with whitewashed panels and a steeply pitched roof. Three small, diamond-paned windows were set deep into its thick walls. The furthest window from the door - fronting what she assumed must be Mr Pepys's makeshift cell - was barred.

A single chimney rose from the lodge, and the flickering orange glow in two of the windows suggested the porter was warming himself by the fire. Abby was glad she had brought a thick woollen blanket, freshly laundered by Betsy.

Knocking thrice on the door, she drew herself to her full height. When nobody answered, she knocked again. Still, there was no response. She tried the handle.

To her surprise, the door opened.

Slumped in a chair, head on chest, gently snoring, was an elderly man with a wiry frame, his thinning grey hair escaping from beneath a well-worn leather cap. A small drool stain had pooled on his white linen shirt.

Glancing around the room - desk with quill, ink, and tankard; ledgers on shelves; pinned notices - Abby's eyes alighted on a set of iron keys hanging from a hook on one wall. At the rear of the room was a hefty, barred wooden door, with a wrought-iron handle and keyhole.

Dare I? she wondered.

As she did so, a familiar face appeared at the bars, looking drawn and grey, with dark circles under the eyes. On seeing her, Pepys's features brightened.

"Abigail!" he cried.

"Hnnn? Wha...?" mumbled the porter, stirring awake and spying Abby. "Who?"

Tutting quietly to herself, Abby marched briskly to the cell door. "His Majesty himself has granted me permission to see Mr Pepys," she said.

"Eh?" replied the porter, clutching at his lower back as he rose from his chair.

"His Majesty has granted me…"

"Aye, aye, I heard all that. I'm not deaf."

"Where have you been?" Pepys hissed to Abby as the porter approached, doddering.

Abby glanced at the porter. "I'm…" she started to say.

"I know who you are, my dear," the porter replied, his tone softly impatient. "I was prepared for your arrival."

Abby declined to point out that he had been asleep.

"My name is Ebenezer Holt," he said when eventually he reached her. "I'm the porter." When she merely pouted, he continued, "Mr Pepys is a fine gentleman. A wealth of most entertaining stories. Are you not, Mr Pepys?"

Pepys raised his eyes to the heavens. "Aye, Ebenezer, that I am."

The old porter sniffed the smoky air. "In all my years at the palace…"

Abby cut him off, "May I…?" she asked, gesturing toward the cell door.

"May you what?"

"Visit Mr Pepys?"

"Aye, mistress. Indeed you may. His Majesty himself did grant…"

"I believe Mistress Harcourt wishes you to unlock the door," urged Pepys, pointing through the bars to the keyhole.

The cell was some 15 feet square, its stone walls at least absorbing a modicum of warmth from the fire next door. Straw on the floor served as bedding, while Abby and Pepys sat beside one another on a short wooden bench – the sole piece of furniture.

Pepys was wearing the same shirt, coat and breeches he had been arrested in, now rumpled and filthy. His wig and hat were gone, and his shorn, dark brown hair clung to his scalp. He was a sorry sight.

Gratefully, he took the blanket Abby offered, wrapped it tight around himself and shuddered. "Where have you been?" he asked again. "And where is Jacob?"

It was the question she had most dreaded. "How fare you?" she asked.

"How do you think I fare, Abigail?" he replied, glaring.

"Mr Holt seems kindly enough?"

"Aye, aye, he is. Were I to be incarcerated, I would wish him as my jailer," he replied, then through gritted teeth added, "*But I do not wish to be incarcerated!*"

"I shall free you, sir, fear not," she said, bowing her head reverentially.

Pepys's ire seemed to fade, and he sighed. "Aye, I trust you will, Abigail. The King visited and explained his predicament. I merely…" He gazed around the cell mournfully. "This situation does not befit me."

"Has your wife, Elizabeth, visited?"

"She is abroad, with her companion," he said, clearly miffed. "What news of your investigation? I long for my home comforts. And where is Jacob?"

She could not avoid the question a second time. "His sister, Anne, is dead. Murdered by the same fiend who took Sophie de Valois's life."

He buried his head in his hands. "Nay," he moaned. "Poor Jacob. How has he taken it?"

Abby could only shake her head.

The young inquisitor went on to summarise, as best she could given the thick web of complications and players, the events of the past couple of days. She lied about the reason for Jacob's absence, saying instead that he had been called away by his mother on an urgent family matter.

"He will return soon," she said, the words emerging brittle.

"Pray, tell me the manner of Jacob's poor sister's demise."

Abby ran a hand through her hair. "The nails were removed from the hinges of her door. Thus, when she opened it…"

Pepys's chin dropped.

"Both mistresses were dispatched by means of sabotage," Abby added. "What can it mean?"

"As my appointed inquisitor, I did hope that you would tell me." There was no anger in his voice, only desperation.

She sighed. "I have but theories for now, sir. The murderer used no weapon; he did not attack, which is the common method of dispatch. It made me wonder: do they not trust their strength?"

"A lady?"

Abby shrugged. "Whoever 'tis, they are cunning."

The two of them sat in silent contemplation as the early-morning sun flooded the small cell, unfettered by the bars on the window.

At length, Pepys asked, "Then where does it leave us?"

She had held off addressing that key question, wary of disappointing her employer. "Do you remember a party held in Anne Standish's honour, at Standish Hall in Greenwich?" she asked. "Ere she entered the King's court? 'Twould have been…"

"Naturally!" he snapped impatiently. "I remember it well. I keep a diary, if you recall?"

"All well in there?" came the porter's croaking voice from the adjacent room.

"Aye, Mr Holt!" Abby chirped back. "Much obliged to you!"

Everything rested on Pepys's reply.

If a single person named on Abby's suspect list - and no others - had attended that event, then they had to be the guilty party. Only they could have stolen Jacob's ring, the same ring that had ended up on the lifeless fingers of both victims.

She began with the courtier highest on her list. "Did Sir William Hakewill attend the party?" she asked.

Pepys pursed his lips and gazed upwards. "Aye!" he replied after an interminable delay, Abby covertly clenching her fists in triumph. "Sir William and I discussed the plague, which had lately come to my notice. He suggested I should not concern myself." He grimaced at the memory.

"Arabella Wyndham?" Abby's features tightened as she silently prayed for a "Nay".

Pepys needed to think only for a second. "Aye," he replied, "she was there. I recall Loxley flirting with her, which she did not seem to mind - the King being elsewhere detained."

Loxley, she was already aware of - but not Arabella.

Hakewill, Loxley, Arabella...

Only one name remained. "Molly Tanner?"

"Nay, Abigail," Pepys chuckled despite his circumstances. "Had Mistress Tanner been present, I daresay we would all have noticed."

And that was that. Her grand plan put into operation - and a single name removed from her suspect list.

It felt like a failure.

Chapter Twenty-Eight

The Bishop's Bosom

In his shattered, bewildered state, Jacob was surprised to find himself simply escorted to the palace exit on White Hall and told gruffly to go home. Abby had pleaded for his life - that much he remembered amid the turmoil. That - and the death of his sister, Anne.

As he reached The Strand in a daze, he glanced around. The streets were empty, save for a few stray hounds and the odd late-night reveller returning home.

With no better plan, he decided to do as he had been told, and return to his townhouse on Strand Lane. The elegant family property was where he lived alone, his mother preferring the rural grandeur of Standish Hall. It had once been owned by Sir William Pride and was given to his father after Pride - who had signed Charles I's death warrant - met his end at the executioner's block.

However, Jacob did not reach the house. Light still glowed in the windows of his local hostelry, The Inn of the Bishop of Chester, as he passed. Drawn by the aroma of hops and tobacco, he decided to drown his troubles in ale.

He knew the place well, often dined there, and considered the landlord, Mr Puddifoot, to be an upstanding gentleman. Adjacent to Somerset House, the richly decorated inn attracted the sort of clientele to whom Jacob could aspire. He felt at ease there.

"Mr Standish! Always a pleasure!" declared Puddifoot, noting Jacob's dishevelled appearance as he entered. "Are we celebrating?"

Jacob pulled up a chair and slumped into it like a sack of coal off a collier's back. "Aye, Mr Puddifoot. That I am. Fetch me ale, would you - and plenty of it." He caught himself cackling strangely as Puddifoot shuffled away.

Am I going mad? he wondered.

Pulling his leather purse from his satchel, the inquisitor weighed it in his hand, the coins inside jingling satisfyingly. *Plenty there to numb the mind*, he thought to himself.

He was not the only patron to register the sound of those coins.

As Jacob looked up, a man took the seat opposite him: a looming fellow with a lustrous periwig and a devilish grin. To Jacob, he seemed the sort who would steal a man's lady and ride off on a stout charger. Since this stranger had no lady, he had nought to fear, he decided.

"Tobias Finch," said the stranger, nodding curtly. "We are not acquainted."

"Nay, sir," Jacob replied. "I am Jacob Standish, personal inquisitor to Mr Samuel Pepys who is…" He hesitated, his usual spiel suddenly deserting him. *What is it that Pepys does?* he wondered.

"I would ask of you a favour, Mr Standish," Finch cut in, his voice smoother than Italian marble, "though it pains me to do so."

"And I feel your pain, sir."

Finch's lips betrayed the hint of a smile. "I was robbed of my purse not half an hour since, outside this very inn. The blackguard took me by surprise, lest I would have…"

Just then, the landlord returned with jug and tankard. Jacob thrust his hand into the air for silence. "Mr Puddifoot, pray fetch a second tankard, would you? I wish to drink with my new friend, Mr…?"

"Finch," said Finch, eyeing the landlord with intent.

Puddifoot stared back, and Finch's hand inched toward his waist, where a glint of steel could be discerned.

"Mr Standish," said Puddifoot, "I would strongly counsel…"

"*Mr Puddifoot,*" Jacob interjected sharply. "*I have requested a second tankard.*"

Ruefully, the landlord shook his head, eyes locked on Finch. "As you wish, sir. But I…"

"I demand the finest ales available to humankind!" Jacob declared, so loudly that others turned and stared. "And I will not be refused!"

"You seem troubled," said Finch, cradling his tankard. "Like a man bearing the weight of the world."

Jacob refilled his own vessel, raised an eyebrow to Finch, who nodded, then did the same for his companion's. Briefly, he considered talking of Anne, but the mere thought of her brought a lump to his throat and he felt himself teeter on the verge of hysteria. Instead, he avoided the subject, settling on the broader strokes of the case.

"I am, sir," he replied with a juddering sigh. "Every path I take, every clue I uncover, leads to the same dead end."

Finch cocked his head. "Every clue, you say?"

"Aye, sir, as I did tell you, I serve as inquisitor to the estimable Mr Pepys."

"And I have never encountered such a trade."

Having bumbled his way through an explanation, Jacob concluded with a flourish, "I can spy a blackguard at a thousand yards!"

Suppressing an arch grin, Finch loosened his cravat. "A rare talent, sir. And, pray, where are you presently inquisiting?"

Jacob straightened himself. "Why, at the King's court, Mr Finch." Returning to his slouch, he took another hearty slug of ale.

Finch raised an eyebrow, unconvinced.

As the warmth of the ale spread through his weary limbs, Jacob grinned stupidly.

Finch reached across the table and slapped him on the arm. "Your work intrigues me, good sir. I would hear more."

In full flow, egged on by the other man, the young inquisitor became most indiscreet. He spoke freely of the death of the King's mistress, Sophie de Valois, her rumoured espionage, and the Standish family ring that had been found upon her finger. He noted how untroubled the King had seemed by her demise.

His tone was ebullient and forceful – until he reached the subject of his fellow inquisitor, Abby, and knew that Anne was not far from the forefront of his tale. By then, the ale that had fired his spirit was clouding his mind, and his thoughts grew grimmer, until he felt once again on the verge of tears.

But Finch only exhorted him for more. "You seem troubled by this Abby, I can tell," he said, sipping at his own drink.

"She believed my sister capable of bloody murder, sir." Jacob laughed bitterly.

"Yet you told me you trust her?"

"With my life." Jacob called for more ale. "Yet now we are estranged," he added, carelessly wiping his eyes with a sleeve.

"I believe I can be of assistance," said Finch.

The inquisitor looked up, blinking blearily at his new companion.

"Can you gain me access to the court?" Finch asked.

Without a word, Jacob dug into his satchel, fumbling as he pulled out a crumpled piece of paper, and passed it across the table.

Finch's eyes widened as he unfolded it. "A warrant of entry to Whitehall Palace. Signed by Sir William Hakewill, no less."

"Friends in high places," Jacob replied, snatching it back.

As he did so, a third man appeared. Garbed in the frills, lace and velvet of an upstanding gentleman, he wore wide-brimmed hat tilted rakishly over the eyes and an expression of wry amusement.

The stranger addressed Finch. "You have a new… acquaintance, I see, Mr Gresham?" He had a noticeable lisp.

Finch shot Jacob a wary glance. "I fear you mistake me for another. My name is Finch," he replied, with a wink that the inquisitor was too befuddled to notice. "Forgive me, I have also forgotten your name, Mr…"

"Albright," offered the other man, grinning. "Thomas Albright. And this is…?"

Jacob gazed up, his eyelids hooded and his eyes bloodshot. "I am Jacob Standish, inquisitor to…" Leering drunkenly, he waved away his own introduction.

"Mr Standish has a purse full of crowns and a warrant of entry to Whitehall Palace," Finch told Albright.

"Does he indeed, Mr Finch?" Albright replied, grinning rotten teeth. "Then perhaps we should discuss the matter with him outside?"

"I believe we should," Finch agreed, rising. "Come, Jacob, some air will do you good."

Gurgling, Jacob swiped his emptied tankard from the table. "I wish only to return home," he muttered.

The landlord appeared among them, beetroot of face, brandishing a ladle in the manner of a club. "I know your game, you scoundrels," he hissed.

Fingering the dagger at his side, Finch leaned down and growled into his ear, "And if you speak one word of it, William Puddifoot, you'll end up dead in the Fleet."

With one arm under each of his, Finch and Albright dragged Jacob away, past his own house - blithely unaware of it - and down into a darkened alcove off Strand Lane. They drew a few glances, but nobody paid them great heed, such drunkenness being no rare sight on London's streets after nightfall.

Finch kicked aside a stray dog, which scuttled away with a whimper, just as the church bell of St Clement Dane's chimed the first stroke of midnight, followed shortly by St Mary-le-Strand's.

Jacob, slumped with his back against a wall, jolted on hearing the familiar peals. "Where am I?" he asked, his voice thick with confusion.

"Hand over the satchel," Finch demanded.

Jacob squinted into the darkness, the two taut, menacing figures blurring before him. "I will not," he mumbled, clutching the bag tightly to his chest.

Finch drew his dagger, its blade glinting in silver moonlight, and took a step forward. "Then you shall die, Jacob Standish."

Chapter Twenty-Nine

Arabella & Son

Arabella Wyndham's lodgings were but a short walk away, back past the Tilt Yard, through the Holbein Gate, down White Hall. If Abby could not dismiss the surliest - and likely most unhinged - of the King's mistresses from her investigation, then she would stand out as a strong suspect.

"Is not Sophie dead?" Those had been Arabella's gloating words in response to her son's accusation that she had lingered too long, unrewarded, in the King's favour. Their stated goals - her covert marriage to Charles and Henry's elevation to a dukedom - would see them rich beyond dreams.

Their deviance stank like the gutters of the city, Abby thought.

And the King was surely aware of it! Given that conversation she had overheard, Arabella had petitioned her royal lover for marriage more than once, only to be spurned each time. Yet she remained neither ousted from the court nor cowed. All that stood between Mistress Wyndham and her desperate ambitions were the other mistresses – and the King's wife, who seemed all too easily forgotten.

"Is not Sophie dead?" The words echoed in Abby's head.

Had Arabella – or even her bastard son by the King – also seen off Anne Standish, she wondered.

Was Molly Tanner's life in peril?

Charles had given her twenty-four hours to find out – and the clock was ticking.

The young manservant who had answered the door the previous day ushered Abby inside. "The mistress is expecting you," he said.

Is she, now? thought the inquisitor. *What games she plays.*

Abby was shown into the study, a curious marriage of Tudor austerity and Restoration elegance. The dark wood panelling of the walls had been brightened with gilded mouldings, and the hefty, arched wooden fireplace now bore a polished marble hearth. The room was softly lit by a multitude of candles, their fragrance – rose oil, perhaps – faint but noticeable.

Arabella Wyndham reclined on a richly upholstered *chaise longue*, draped in a billowing gown of regal-red silk edged with lace. Her *décolletage* was daringly low, while her loosely curled black hair spilled artfully around her shoulders. She wore a smile, coquettish and teasing, as though savouring the exchange yet to unfold.

Behind her stood Henry, whom Abby disliked on sight. In his mid-teens, with wavy blond hair, he stood with arms folded, exuding contempt. Dressed in gold-embroidered finery better suited to a prince than to such a charlatan, he was vanity writ large.

"At last, the maid arrives!" he said, laughing at his own wit. His voice was nasal, its pitch torn somewhere between boy and man.

Arabella's expression did not change.

"I'm wise to you," said Abby, wishing her hands would cease fidgeting.

"You are nervous," Arabella replied. "Why?"

"I know your plan."

"Do I unsettle you?"

Aye, thought Abby. "I am Mr Samuel Pepys's personal inquisitor…"

"Would that be," the boy cut her off, "the same Samuel Pepys who presently resides in the court jail?"

"And would you be the same Henry Wyndham who clings to his mother's skirts, bleating for legitimacy?"

"Ha!" Henry barked. "I…"

"Hush!" Arabella barked, rising to a seated position. "I will speak with this… girl."

Abby snorted softly at the insult, but her hands refused to be stilled.

"Does the sting of your tongue match that of your mind, Abigail?" Arabella asked. "I wonder… Whom do you suspect of Sophie's murder? In whose mind does such evil lurk?"

"In yours, Arabella?" Abby shot back, quick as a flash. "Or does your son carry out your ungodly bidding?"

Henry stamped his foot, his face flushing scarlet. "Mother, cast out the impudent wench, she…"

Once again, his mother cut him off. "I said, 'Hush,' Henry!" Turning to the inquisitor, she told her, "You are the dilettante I suspected, my dear, and no match for any villain."

Abby detected a curious undertone to her voice. *Is it… dismay?* She wondered. *Or even fear?* "Then whom do you suspect?" she asked.

Arabella rose gracefully and began walking toward the inquisitor. "Hakewill loathes us," she said; Abby presumed she was referring to the King's mistresses. "And I hear talk of his thievery."

Abby said nothing, hoping to conceal her surprise.

Halting a few feet short of her, Arabella shrugged. "I trust him not. 'Tis said his wife, Lady Charlotte, died in suspicious circumstances."

Abby held her gaze, unwittingly transfixed, waiting for her to elaborate.

"She fell from her horse. 'Twas claimed her bridle had been loosened."

Arabella moved away, her robe trailing behind her along the polished wooden floor, almost giving the impression that she was floating. Hers was a rare beauty, though fading.

Abby had learned of the woman through Pepys.

Arabella Somerville was born into a well-connected royalist family in 1630. When her father died fighting for King Charles I during the first Civil War, it left the family financially strained. Ambitious and strikingly attractive, Arabella resolved to use her charm, wit and looks to secure a wealthy husband.

In 1647, she wed Robert Wyndham, educated at Eton and Cambridge, a Member of Parliament whose substantial income derived primarily from inherited estates. The marriage was tumultuous from the very beginning, thanks largely to Arabella's openly scandalous behaviour and burgeoning reputation for infidelity.

Such brazen defiance of convention only heightened her allure, and it was inevitable she would one day catch the eye of the similarly louche King Charles II. Her charisma and boldness captivated His Majesty, who made her his mistress despite her marriage. Their son, Henry, was born out of wedlock in 1651.

(Robert was placated with an honorary earldom; whether his esteem ever recovered was debatable.)

Arabella's influence over Charles was immense; she used her charm and cunning to outwit rivals, amassing a fortune in the process, for which she remained unapologetic.

Yet there was something in her tone that day, some chink in her armour perhaps, that the inquisitor could not yet place.

Abby and Henry watched as she stood before a large, gilt-framed mirror, admiring herself. Idly lifting strings of pearls from her neck, she watching them fall back into place with a soft clatter.

At length, she spoke. "Charles tells me Anne Standish has fled the palace, in fear for her life."

So that's how he explains her absence, Abby thought. "I'm unaware of such," she replied.

"If you know so little," Arabella's gaze remained fixed on her own reflection, "then why are you here?"

"To uncover Sophie's murderer and bring him to justice."

"You assume 'tis a man?"

Abby cursed her careless tongue. "It may be a lady." She paused. "It may even be you."

"How so?" Arabella's tone remained unruffled.

"You wish to wed the King in secret, to become Queen. It would greatly assist your purpose, were the other mistresses conveniently removed."

Arabella swivelled angrily, while her son stared on in horror. "Who told you this?" she snarled.

Abby allowed herself a small, victorious smile.

"Mother!" yelped the boy.

Arabella stormed across the room, her face stopping inches from Abby's. Her scent was undeniably exquisite. *"I said, who told you this?"*

"Only the King himself knows," Henry gasped.

"Be silent!" Arabella thundered, her rage dominating the room, which was how she liked it. Returning her attention to Abby, she demanded, "Who else knows?"

"Nobody."

Arabella's piercing brown eyes flicked between Abby's, seeking out deceit. The inquisitor calmly returned her gaze. Gradually, Arabella's features softened. "You tell the truth."

"I always do," Abby lied.

From nowhere, Arabella reached for Abby's hand, squeezing it tightly. Her mask slipped, and a different woman appeared - one who was not of the court, nor obsessed with riches and power, but frail and anxious. "Am I to be next?" she asked.

Abby frowned.

"The next victim of this devil who stalks the palace," Arabella elaborated urgently.

Is that fear in her eyes? wondered Abby. "I should go," she said. "I must leave the palace tonight."

Arabella let Abby's hand drop. "But… why on earth, when the devil remains at large?"

"On the King's orders."

She smacked her palms together angrily. "Charles is a fool!"

Abby turned to leave. "Yet he denies you your devious plot."

"In truth," Henry piped up, haughtily, "he accedes to our wishes. We were informed only this morning, I am to become Duke of Roscommon. Thus, our *devious plot*, as you deem it, is gaining pace. His Majesty stages a lavish masque in my honour on the morrow, for his most esteemed courtiers to attend. Then our triumph shall be evident to all."

Chapter Thirty

The Visitor

The investigation was slipping through Abby's fingers. As she walked up White Hall toward the Holbein Gate, her mind churned with possibilities.

Had that been genuine fear in Arabella's face? If so, it would be hard to believe she was the murderer. Or was she playing a shrewd and cunning game? Of all the suspects, Arabella seemed to have the most to gain from the deaths of the other mistresses.

And what of Molly? Abby struggled to imagine her capable of such atrocities. She was too gentle, too vivacious, too open. Molly had not attended Anne Standish's party and so could not have stolen the ring. Yet, considering it now, might there have been other ways for her to gain access to it?

Molly was no flighty nincompoop - despite what the men might perceive - and acting was, after all, her talent. Might she have acquired the ring from whomever had taken it from Jacob?

Abby groaned inwardly. Her suspect list simply refused to grow shorter.

As for Loxley, he surely had reason to murder Sophie de Valois, to spite both her and the King for cuckolding him. But why then murder Anne Standish? Abby had found no apparent motive… of which, she was painfully aware. It did not mean there was none.

Finally, Sir William Hakewill, the King's trusted adviser. An overbearing man who openly despised the mistresses, and whose wife had perished in a fall from her horse. Whispers now trailed Hakewill like chains, hinting at foul play in her death and of alleged thievery. Yet both rumours stemmed from the same source: Arabella Wyndham - who might have very good reason to deflect guilt onto another.

Abby dug her fingernails into her palms, the sharp pain grounding her frustration. She fought against the urge to cry out. The sense that she did not belong in this gilded labyrinth had clung to her since she first set foot in it. None, from His Majesty downward, seemed to regard her in earnest.

If only she could solve this mystery. Then the King might look upon her with favour, he could pardon Mr Pepys, and his dreadful courtiers would have no choice but to grant her the respect she deserved.

A bell tolled across the rooftops. Abby listened as it rang once, twice, then fell silent. *Two of the clock*, she thought, once again quelling the raw, animal cry that threatened to escape her cracked lips.

Where now? she wondered, knowing that time was of the essence.

How she missed Jacob. While she sympathised with his plight, she was also beginning to feel let down. They were inquisitors together, effective as a team – at least, until now. But separate… That was proving to be an altogether different kettle of fish.

Roused from her musings, Abby realised she had retraced the familiar route to her lodgings and found herself outside Anne Standish's house. The windows were dark, the candles within extinguished, and the place silent. The property was empty.

Empty, she thought, trying the door. *What secrets still lie in there?*

The last time she had tried to search the place, the King had disturbed her - and she felt she had sensed Hakewill's presence.

When the door would not budge, she barged the heavy oak in frustration, sending a sharp pain down her arm.

Clutching at it, cursing under her breath, she caught a noise - the rattling of a door handle - at the end of the street. Instinctively, she ducked into the narrow alleyway between Anne's and Molly Tanner's properties.

Quick footsteps followed, drawing closer, and she pressed herself into the shadows. Peering out, Abby spied none other than Sir William himself, striding past with what appeared to be a painting shrouded in cloth.

Might the rumours be true? she wondered. *Is he a thief?*

The house Hakewill had exited stood beyond Molly's, set perpendicular to it at a confluence of streets. Abby had noticed it before – grander than Molly and Anne's houses, with renovations and refinements more akin to Arabella's lodgings. The tall windows were flanked by delicately carved stone pilasters, and there were smaller, arched windows projecting outward from the roof. It was a feature she had never seen before.

Now, she wondered who lived there.

The windows were shuttered, offering no hint of an inhabitant, so Abby tentatively knocked.

Pressing her ear to the door, she heard nothing.

This place feels abandoned, she reassured herself and, conscious of the keyhole, reached for the handle.

To her surprise, the door swung open.

The entrance hall was unlit; Abby hurriedly closed the door behind her, immersing herself in darkness and silence. In the fleeting moment before it shut, she caught sight of a small table by the door, upon which sat a candle and lighting implements. Stumbling forward in hesitant, uneven steps, she stretched out her hands, seeking the reassuring touch of the wood.

Her fingers brushed the table's edge, then found the smooth wax cylinder of the candle. A short while later, a tiny flame flickered to life, casting a ghostly glow.

The vast tapestries lining the hallway loomed large in the wavering light, their scale almost overwhelming. Now, with only the sound of her own breathing for company, Abby could take in their splendour. Palaces sprawled across expansive landscapes in the intricate weavings, where nobles hunted deer and boar. Yet these were no English palaces, she realised.

On another wall-hanging, shimmering with gold and silver thread, she recognised the unmistakable figure of the Sun King: Louis XIV, ruler of France.

The decor was undeniably French. This was Mistress Sophie de Valois's former residence, now abandoned, cold, and unwelcoming.

Then what, she wondered, *was Hakewill's business here?*

At the opposite end of the hallway, Abby made out a wide staircase curving upwards to both the right and left. She resolved to seek out Sophie's chamber, where her jewellery was likely kept. While paintings were generally rather bulky to pilfer - which may not have stopped Hakewill taking the more compact ones - precious metals and stones were not.

Creeping up the polished wooden stairs, one hand gliding along the wide, smooth rail, Abby was struck by the enormity of the space. Gilt-framed portraits lined the walls, their subjects' beady eyes glaring down at her accusingly. So heightened were her senses that she fancied she could almost hear their whispered outrage.

At the top, the symmetrical staircases merged into a wide balcony, leading to another hallway. At its far end, a stained-glass window loomed dark and muted, its vibrant colours subdued in the absence of daylight, leaving only faint, shadowed patterns across the floor.

This first-floor hallway was lined with more tapestries and doors, one of which Abby knew must lead to Sophie's chamber. Already tense, she steeled herself to open the first door when a noise reached her ears: a low rattle, followed by a faint thump, as though coming from the street outside.

Could be anything, she thought, trying to calm her overstretched nerves.

Then came another sound - of footsteps ascending the staircase below.

Although Abby could not see over the balcony from where she stood, the sound of the interloper's wheezing breaths confirmed what she already suspected.

Hakewill had returned.

Suppressing a cry of alarm, she opened the door to find an imposing four-poster bed and walls lined with furniture and portraiture.

But there was no time to linger. Stepping swiftly inside, she gingerly closed the door and hurried toward a towering walnut armoire, guided by her candlelight.

Opening its double doors, she found expensive gowns draped from a horizontal rail. With a gentle puff, she blew out her candle and stepped inside. Forcing her way through the embroidered fabrics, aware of lavender and dust, she reached out to pull the doors shut.

And there she stood, frozen, concealed behind Mistress de Valois's exquisite garments, barely daring to breathe.

Did he hear me? she wondered.

Hakewill made straight for the chamber where Abby was hiding, swung open the door, and, from what she could gather, stood there surveying the scene.

Is he hunting me down? she wondered, clutching her fists tight to her chest. Her heart thudded in her ears, until it seemed to her like a crashing drumbeat, betraying her hiding place.

She heard him step into the room. "Now," he said, with what sounded like the rubbing of his hands. "The jewels, methinks."

His footsteps approached, and she tensed further, but he stopped short of her armoire. She heard drawers opening and slamming shut, accompanied by Hakewill's muttered agitation.

It did not take long for him to find what he was looking for, when the room fell briefly silent. "Ah!" he gasped, followed by the soft creak of another lid being lifted. "And still more." Then, to the sound of necklaces being lifted by the handful, he began grumbling to himself in a low voice.

"Such wanton whores. No virtue, no modesty - only greed and indulgence." His words dripped with scorn as he rifled through the treasures. "Gifts from a blind king who ignores my warnings and rewards corruption."

He paused, perhaps eyeing some ridiculously expensive, glittering bauble. "Well may they preen and flaunt their ill-gotten riches, yet now," his tone darkened, "they reap the fruits of their own wickedness. And who shall fall next, I wonder? The false queen-in-waiting or the playhouse strumpet?"

Once again, silence descended, so eerie it felt suffocating.

Then suddenly, the doors to the armoire were wrenched open. It was all Abby could do not to cry out. She dared not move a muscle.

Before her very eyes, a podgy, ringed hand reached in and tugged at a damask robe hanging mere inches from her face. She could see the ink stains on Hakewill's fingers and held her breath, terrified he would sense her presence.

"These will fetch a precious penny," he muttered, thrusting the robe back with a grunt. The jangle of jewellery sounded as he shifted his ill-gotten gains. "Patience is a virtue. I shall act on the morrow."

With that, he closed the armoire doors and left the room, his footsteps fading into the hallway.

Chapter Thirty-One

Threat

It was several long minutes before Abby dared to move a muscle. The air inside the armoire was thick with dust, and though she longed to sneeze, she managed to stifle it. The tension had been unbearable, leaving her drained and sweating.

At last, long after she heard what sounded like the closing of the main entrance door, she pushed the robes aside and eased herself out of the armoire. A part of her expected Hakewill to be standing there, waiting to grab her by the throat and throttle the life from her.

But that's not his way, is it? she assured herself. *Hakewill favours sabotage.*

Abby fled from Sophie's lodgings as if the Devil himself were at her heels. So unsettled was she that she collided headlong with Molly Tanner, who was just stepping out of her own apartment.

"Whoa, missy!" Molly exclaimed, flailing to keep her balance. "What's the hurry?"

The inquisitor clutched her face in both hands, looking fit to faint.

"Nay," Molly said soothingly, rubbing her back. "What troubles you?"

When Abby did not reply, merely shaking her head in dumb dismay, Molly guided her into her lodgings.

Mistress Tanner's parlour was considerably less ostentatious than those of her rivals, and more homely - though the silver candlesticks, bronze sculptures and delicate porcelain ornaments suggested she was never far from the King's thoughts.

The walls were covered in playbills, and Abby noticed a few printed with Molly's name, from the Theatre Royal, Drury Lane. Among them, The Indian Emperour by John Dryden, The Humorous Lieutenant by John Fletcher, and The English Monsieur by James Howard.

Molly made them some tea, set Abby's cup before her, and sat beside her at a large table. In its centre was a fruit bowl, perhaps an ironic reminder of the actor's impoverished past.

"You don't have servants?" Abby asked, inhaling the calming scent of her drink.

Molly laughed. "Nay! All those prying eyes. My business is my business."

They sat in silence while Molly stroked the inquisitor's hair.

"What were you doing in Sophie's apartment?" she asked at length.

Abby stared into her pale blue eyes. *Can I trust her?* she wondered, and it struck her: without Jacob by her side, who else could she turn to?

She exhaled. "Arabella told me that Hakewill's a thief, and 'tis true," she blurted out. "I heard him steal Sophie's jewels with my own ears…"

"But you didn't see him?"

"I was hiding… It matters not." Abby grasped Molly's hand. "Hakewill asked himself which of the King's mistresses would perish next, Molly. You or Arabella." She shuddered at the memory.

The young actor only seemed amused. "What of Anne Standish?"

"You heard nought last night?"

"I was away, at Drury Lane," Molly replied, pointing to the Indian Emperour playbill. "Delighting my multitude of admirers! Oh, Abigail, you should have been there, 'twas…"

The inquisitor cut her off. "Anne's dead - slain by the same callous hand that took Sophie's life."

Molly froze, gaze fixed on Abby, searching desperately for some sign that this was a macabre jest. It quickly became clear that it was not.

Abby gripped Molly's hand so tightly that her knuckles whitened. "The King made me swear I would breathe not a word of Anne's death to a soul. You mustn't let on."

Molly offered a grim smile and pressed a hand to her chest. "You have my word."

"I fear for you, Molly," Abby said urgently. "I believe Hakewill is coming for you, and that he will act soon."

Molly seemed unsure whether to laugh or cry. "Soon?" she asked. "At the masque, perchance?"

Abby's jaw tightened. *The celebration in honour of Arabella's runt-son.* "At the masque!" she echoed, realisation dawning. *It would cause such a scene.*

Molly shook her head disbelievingly. "You think Sir William murdered Sophie?"

"I'm sure of it."

Molly snorted. "Nay, Abigail. The oaf is too idle and lumpish. He lacks the vigour for murder."

"'Tis why he uses sabotage!"

The young mistress pulled her hand away from Abby's. "What proof do you have?"

"I witnessed his thieving!"

"And his murdering?"

"He murders that he may thieve!"

"I ask again, Abigail, what proof do you have?" When Abby offered no response, she added, "By the by, where is your tall male accomplice? Has he deserted you?"

Abby blinked.

"You're better off without him," Molly said, her tone softening. "He didn't seem terribly bright."

The inquisitor fixed Molly's gaze. "Never judge a book by its cover."

Rising, the young actor laughed wryly. "I never would, Abigail. Since I cannot read."

As she was taking her leave, Abby found a piece of paper thrust into her hand.

"I received this only today," Molly told her. "'Twas pushed 'neath my door. I paid it little heed, yet I did wonder what it said."

Abby read aloud:

Molly lies in shallow waters. Tread carefully or she will flounder.

Molly gasped, the colour draining from her cheeks. "A threat?"

The inquisitor, however, was already scrutinising the note. "See here – two words have been crossed through before 'Tread carefully…' And the name has been altered. It once read…" She peered closely at the handwriting. "It once read 'Mary.'"

"What words were crossed through?"

"It looks like, 'We must…'" Abby replied. "This note originally read, 'Mary lies in shallow waters. We must tread carefully, or she will flounder.' Whoever passed it to you altered its meaning. Aye, Molly, 'tis a threat. Sophie de Valois received a similar note."

The young actor's earlier amusement vanished. "Who the hell is Mary?"

Abby had no answer.

"And you believe my life is in danger?" Molly asked.

Abby sighed. "As I told you."

Molly's face hardened into a grim resolve. "I can look after myself," she said. "For it has ever been the way."

With that, she turned on her heel and strode toward the stairs, leaving the inquisitor to find her own way out.

Chapter Thirty-Two

Red Mist

It was dusk by the time Abby returned to her apartment, painfully aware that her time at the palace was all but spent. She would plead with the King, she decided. Once he knew how close she was to solving the crime, he would surely prolong her stay.

But dare I name Hakewill? she wondered.

It was one thing to confide her suspicions to Molly Tanner; quite another to accuse the King's trusted adviser of murder.

"What proof do you have?" Molly's words rang in her ears.

Hakewill despised the mistresses, she assured herself. If he needed to steal to maintain his lavish lifestyle, then who better to target than those obscenely wealthy women? And he could only thieve from them once they were gone.

It has to be him, she thought.

If only she could prove it.

Had Jacob been at her side, he would have spotted something – a clue she had overlooked.

Molly was right. He had deserted her. Just as he had deserted his dear Anne, who now lay cold in her grave.

Men. They were all the same – grown boys cloaked in self-importance, blind to the needs and emotions of others.

All at once, the pressures of her days at court seemed to converge, crushing her very soul. Crying out to the rafters in anguish, she stormed upstairs toward her room.

So blinded by fury was she that she failed to notice the balled blanket lying on one of the uppermost steps. As her foot sank into it, the fabric unfurled beneath her, sending her reeling backward.

"Mistress!"

Abby was only dimly aware of the maid's shriek as she tumbled down the hard wooden stairs, colliding with step after step, until she came to a halt on the floor below.

And there she lay.

Motionless

Chapter Thirty-Three

Revival

When Jacob came to, his mouth tasted of stale ash and his head pounded like a cartwheel over cobblestones. *Where am I?* he wondered. *And what happened to me?*

It felt as though he were in bed. Nervously, he conducted a cursory examination with wandering fingertips - the only part of him that could be willed to move. The blanket felt familiar… and he appeared to be fully clothed.

Opening his right eyelid, he saw only gloom. The left followed, and he turned his head towards a faint orange haze - street-light spilling through shutters. *Those are my shutters*, he thought.

It gradually dawned on him that he was in his own bedroom, on Strand Lane.

But how on earth had he got there?

Suddenly, he heard the door flung open and a voice - a familiar voice - call out, "Mr Standish! I heard you stir!"

Jacob shifted position, scrutinising the figure out-lined in the doorway. "Quigley?"

"One and the same, sir!" replied the old coney-catcher, bounding into the room to wrap the inquisitor in a crushing embrace.

"Leave me be!" Jacob protested, now fully awake and aware of a stabbing pain at his temple. Reaching up, he felt a large lump there. "What happened to me?"

The pair had encountered one another before. Jim Quigley - master of disguise, common thief and gen-eral reprobate - had helped the inquisitors in their previous investigation within London's coffee houses. While Jacob had not always relished the old man's involvement, having been rather easily conned by him during their initial meeting, he was painfully aware that their success had owed much to Quigley's dubious talents.

As Quigley plonked himself down on the foot of the bed, Jacob sat up indignantly. "You'd be dead without me," said Quigley matter-of-factly.

A mist of disjointed memories swirled through Ja-cob's mind: too many tankards of ale, a tall gentleman with a soothing voice yet darkness behind his eyes, Mr Puddifoot… *clutching a ladle?*

"You crossed paths with Danny Gresham," Quigley went on. "A most dangerous individual."

Jacob felt again for the lump on his head. "He did attack me?"

Quigley chuckled. "Nay, Mr Standish. You were unsteady on your feet as I helped you home, and you struck the door with your head."

That roused the inquisitor. "What nonsense!" He retorted. "I know nought of this Gresham fellow!"

"I believe he called himself Finch?"

The name rang the smallest of bells.

"Just as I called myself Albright," Quigley added.

Albright? Albright? Albright? thought Jacob. "The gentlemen with the lisp?"

"One and the ttthh...ame," quipped the coney-catcher, exaggerating the style.

"And... and this other man? Gresham?"

"Dead in the Fleet, sir."

Jacob only heard the first of those words, and the painful memory hit him. "My darling Anne," he muttered forlornly.

The two repaired to Jacob's parlour, where they had once planned their bold assault on the Palace of Westminster. Quigley produced a flagon of ale, the sight of which made Jacob's stomach churn. Yet, in the absence of quaffable water, he was obliged to partake to quench his seething thirst.

"What hour is it?" Jacob asked. "How long have I slept?"

"For nigh on one full day, Mr Standish. You were very much the worse for wear."

Thrusting his head into his hands, Jacob groaned. *What of Abby?* he wondered. *Left all alone at the court to solve his sister's murder, desperate for my assistance.* Then he remembered: *And Mr Pepys.* "I am such an ass," he moaned aloud.

"May I assist, sir?" asked Quigley, pulling out a gold pocket watch engraved - quite clearly - with another man's name. "I have time on my hands."

Jacob poured forth the emotions that had haunted even his dreams. He recounted the terrible sight of his sister's pale hand, their shared childhoods, his suspicions surrounding her death, the earlier murder of Sophie de Valois, and the growing list of suspects.

Quigley listened with rapt attention, occasionally prompting Jacob to repeat certain details or coaxing more clarity from his muddled recollections. At last, when he seemed satisfied, he declared, "The truth lies within, Mr Standish. 'Tis for you to decipher, and I trust you will. Use your inquisitor's instinct."

Jacob was unconvinced.

"I trust in you, sir," Quigley said gently. "Did you not save the King's life?"

Jacob nodded slowly, finding himself warming to the old scoundrel. "I must return to the palace forthwith," he announced, rising to leave, and buckling under a fresh pain in one knee.

Quigley stayed him with a hand. "Nay, sir. You're bloodied, and your thoughts remain shrouded in mist. Sleep again, and wake with a clearer head. You will need your wits about you, come morning."

Sensing the wisdom in the old man's words, Jacob retook his seat.

Quigley tapped his flagon, winking. "But first, we finish my ale." Ignoring Jacob's theatrical wince, he added. "I would hear your tales of court once again."

Chapter Thirty-Four

The Name of the King

"Oh, thank the Lord," Abby heard, as her eyelids fluttered open. She was in her bed at court, that much she could discern.

Betsy Underwood's blurred face loomed over her, strands of the servant's untied hair resting on her cheek and tickling her nose. As Abby lifted her arm to brush them aside, a sharp pain shot through her elbow, and she let out a strangled yelp.

"What happened?" Abby asked, though her spinning mind was already piecing it together. Her whole body seemed to ache.

Betsy, dabbing a damp cloth on her forehead, drew a long sigh. "Can you forgive me, mistress? I had no idea you were in the house till I heard you cry out below. I'd left the…"

"Blanket," Abby cut in. "On the stairs."

"I'd left the blanket on the stairs to be laundered, mistress. I…"

Gingerly raising her arm, Abby pressed a finger to Betsy's lips. Her sleeve slipped down as she did so, revealing angry bruising on her forearm. "Hush," she said. "Help me up."

"But mistress, you must rest! You took a terrible tumble."

Ignoring the maid's protestations, Abby shifted herself to the side of the bed and sat up. To her great relief, no limbs appeared to be broken, though her elbows and knees were mottled purple-black. Her lower lip was cut and swollen, and she could feel a welt on the top of her head, hidden beneath her hair.

She would just about pass muster, she felt.

Betsy could only stare in anguish. "Mistress Harcourt…"

"I've no time to waste," Abby said, shifting her weight onto her feet and standing unsteadily. "Come, help me down the stairs."

A loud banging came on the door below. "Open up!" commanded the rasping male voice.

The two young women exchanged wide-eyed glances.

"Open this door, in the name of the King!"

Squeezing Abby's wrist, Betsy ran for the stairs.

When she returned, her face fell. "You're to leave at once," she told Abby. "A wherry awaits you at the Privy Stairs."

Abby sank back onto the bed and buried her face in her hands. "I've failed," she groaned. "Mr Pepys will never forgive me, and a murderer remains at large in Whitehall, set to claim another victim. I've failed," she repeated, barely above a whisper.

She felt the mattress beside her sag, and Betsy's arm around her shoulders.

"'Tis vital you remain here?" the servant asked.

Abby could barely manage a nod.

"Against the King's orders?" Betsy pressed.

Abby shrugged wearily.

"I have a plan," said the maid.

Chapter Thirty-Five

Jonas Cuttle

Instead of heading towards the mistresses' apartments, Abby turned sharply to the right, back towards the Privy Stairs - the very route she, Jacob and Pepys had taken on the day they arrived. It felt like a lifetime ago, though in truth it had been only a matter of days.

Hobbling awkwardly, escorted by a guard who had arrived at her lodgings as she prepared to leave, Abby felt every ache of her battered body.

Night had fallen, and even in this well-heeled quarter of London, the sound of stray dogs barking and tussling carried through the bitingly cold air. Smoke from a multitude of chimneys veiled the moon in thin clouds.

As she passed the King's apartments, a door creaked open and there he stood: Charles, wearing little more than a nightshirt and a rakish smile. His head was bare of periwig, and his dark brown eyes sparkled with mischief despite the late hour.

He offered her his outstretched hand, which she dutifully kissed. "I did wish to see you, Mistress Harcourt, ere you departed," he said. "Your efforts here have been greatly appreciated, if, alas, the task has proven beyond your capabilities."

'Tis true, she was bold enough to admit to herself, and the admission stung. She briefly considered pleading for more time - but there was no bargaining with a monarch. "I only wish I could have served Your Majesty with greater success," she said quietly.

Smiling sympathetically, he took her hand and touched his cold lips against her pale knuckles. "Goodbye, Abigail," he said, and was gone.

No invitation to return, she noted. *If only he knew.*

At the foot of the Privy Stairs, a small wherry was waiting. A lone oarsman stood at the prow, his face obscured beneath a wide-brimmed hat. The night was still, barely a breeze; the Thames stretched before Abby, silvery and calm, disrupted only by the light passage of the nightly river traffic.

"Jonas Cuttle?" she asked hesitantly. Were it not him, the plan would fail at the first hurdle.

"Aye, mistress," came the reply. "I'm Cuttle."

As she stepped into the boat, helped by the waterman, she glanced up towards her escort. He had not left, but remained atop the stairs, watching.

He was still there as Cuttle cast off and began rowing them downriver. Head bowed, she watched him surreptitiously as they drifted away from Whitehall Palace, not daring to move, lest she arouse suspicion.

Only when the wherry reached mid-river, heading north toward the heart of the city, did the guard finally turn on his heel and disappear among the royal buildings.

"You know the plan?" Abby asked Cuttle, leaning forward on her wooden bench.

"Plan, mistress?" he replied, not breaking his rhythm.

Her heart sank. "Didn't Betsy Underwood speak with you? She told me she knows you?"

The waterman lifted his oars from the water. A smile cracked beneath the shadow of his hat brim. "I'm jesting," he said.

As Cuttle turned the boat about, Abby cast a nervous glance toward the shore. So many palace buildings lined the river; she might be spotted at any moment. She re-assured herself that most of the windows were shrouded in darkness, their occupants likely asleep. It calmed her - somewhat.

The waterman rowed them steadily past the Privy Stairs, keeping them mid-river among the other few wherries present, to avoid drawing attention. Abby, al-ready small, made herself even smaller, stooped and hud-dled.

The high, austere Tudor walls of the palace loomed to her right, as if they were watchful sentinels, alert to her subterfuge but powerless to act.

The journey seemed to take forever, and Abby silently willed Cuttle to row faster. Relief washed over her when finally she spotted a familiar silhouette at the foot of a short flight of steps up ahead, beckoning urgently.

"Hurry!" Betsy urged, as the little wherry glided toward the riverbank.

These stairs, the servant had explained, were reserved for the King himself, ferrying ladies to his nightly assignations. As such, they remained unguarded - deliberately avoided by the palace attendants.

"Come!" Betsy urged, leading Abby up darkened steps. At the top, Abby paused, her gaze drawn across an expansive, meticulously tended lawn she realised must be the Bowling Green. To her right, a tall stone building loomed, several of its many windows flickering with candlelight.

Betsy gestured for Abby to crouch down out of sight, as they crept deeper into the palace. "The Groom of the Bedchamber's lodgings," she whispered close to Abby's ear. "He's likely awake."

Amid the stark tension, the inquisitor had all but forgotten her injuries. Yet, in the back of her mind, she remained acutely aware: her punishment if discovered here would be severe. Far worse than any fall down a flight of stairs.

Having skirted the Groom's residence, Abby straightened to her full height and paused before the first door she encountered. Betsy pulled her away. "Not that one," she whispered. "It leads to the Stone Gallery. There'll be guards."

Instead, the servant moved ahead to another door just a few yards further on. There she stopped, and called out softly, "Lizzy?"

When no reply came, she tapped the wood lightly. *"Lizzy?"*

The door creaked open, revealing a young servant whose face was rigid with apprehension. At the sight of Betsy and Abby, her expression softened, and she pulled the door fully open. "Quickly!" Lizzy whispered, ushering them inside.

Instantly, Abby recognised the Privy Garden, its marble statutes glowing like ghosts beneath the moonlight.

Hugging the wall, the three young women quickly covered the length of the garden, when Abby found herself in familiar territory. Without a word, Lizzy took her leave, walking steadily in the direction of Banqueting House.

With a sharp nod, Betsy led the way toward Anne Standish and Molly Tanner's lodgings. Passing them undetected - their windows dark - they were suddenly startled by the sound of heavy footsteps echoing in their direction.

Panicked, they froze, staring at one another in silent horror as the steps grew relentlessly louder. Betsy's eyes darted about until she spotted a covered porch. Without hesitation, she pushed Abby inside just as a palace guard rounded the corner.

"Who goes there?" the guard barked, halting abruptly as he drew his sword.

"George?" Betsy ventured, her voice noticeably quivering. "George Carter?"

"Betsy? What are you doing out at this hour?"

"Why, I couldn't sleep," she replied, "so I took a stroll."

Abby noticed the hem of her robe spilling out into the street and swiftly tugged it back into the doorway.

The guard stepped closer to Betsy. "'Tis mighty untoward, wandering so late," he told her, eyebrow arched.

She giggled coquettishly. "The night is far too lovely to waste indoors."

"Not for a palace guard, 'tis not," he replied, and continued on his way.

As Abby and Betsy neared the lodgings of the Queen's Maids of Honour, situated just across the courtyard from the inquisitor's former residence, a face appeared briefly at one of the windows. Moments later, the door opened, revealing the matronly woman Abby had once spoken with. Clad in a white nightdress and clutching a lantern, she peered out at them.

"Quickly!" she urged.

Abby turned to thank Betsy, but the young servant was already disappearing inside her own lodgings.

"Come!" the Queen's maid hissed, beckoning urgently.

Abby slipped inside, and the door closed behind her.

She was back in the heart of the royal palace.

Chapter Thirty-Six

The Vanishing

Abby slept soundly that night and woke to the sound of a maidservant placing a goblet of small ale beside her. Her truckle bed had proved comfortable, with a thick woollen blanket keeping the chill at bay.

As she sat up, her gaze drifted to the three other beds in the room, identical to hers - each empty and neatly made.

"What hour is this?" she asked.

The maid, her black hair tucked beneath a crisp linen coif, merely shook her head. Before Abby could repeat the question, the woman who had greeted her the previous night entered the dormitory.

"She cannot understand you," she said. "Like Her Majesty, she is Portuguese."

The maid smiled, nodded graciously, and left the room.

In that moment, Abby felt an unfamiliar but welcome sense of sanctity.

Abby's saviour identified herself as Agnes Ashcombe, Mistress of the Maids. Her silver-streaked hair was tucked neatly beneath a lace-edged coif. She wore a modest yet well-tailored gown of dark blue wool, with a high neckline and simple embroidered cuffs. A ring of keys hung from a belt at her waist.

Kindly yet steadfast, she bore an air of brusque efficiency.

"The masque begins at noon in the Great Hall. We must prepare you," she told Abby, and began rooting in a chest of drawers.

Unable to contain her curiosity, Abby asked, "Why are you helping me?"

Agnes paused and studied the inquisitor's face. "Ladies are dying, Abigail," she replied with a hint of incredulity, and returned to her work.

As the inquisitor threw off her blanket, she noticed she was wearing only her undergarments. Without looking up, Agnes told her softly, "You fell sound asleep."

Abby sat up. "I'm a little confused," she said. "I'm to attend the masque dressed as a servant?" When Agnes failed to reply, she continued, "But my face is known – even to the King himself. I'll surely be recognised."

Clutching a small bundle of clothing, Agnes closed the drawer and turned to face the inquisitor. "Abigail, 'tis the perfect disguise. No one here spares a thought for the servants. We are invisible."

Abby donned the uniform of Queen Catherine's Maids of Honour: a dove-grey silk skirt and a black fitted bodice with a lace-trimmed neckline. The inquisitor's distinctive red hair was pinned into a tight bun and concealed beneath a coif.

Agnes stood back and looked her up and down. Nodding to herself, she declared briskly, "Now we must feed you. 'Twill be a long day."

As the Mistress of Maids turned on her heel, a thought occurred to Abby. "What if somebody recognises my voice?" she asked, hurrying to keep pace.

Without breaking stride, the Mistress replied. "Most of the Queen's maids are Portuguese. If a gentleman addresses you, you simply reply, 'Eu não entendo'."

"I don't understand," Abby replied, unfamiliar with the language.

"Precisely, my dear."

Chapter Thirty-Seven

The Great Hall

Abby joined a line of Maids of Honour, identically dressed but of varying heights - she one of the smallest - processing toward the Great Hall. Overhead, the sky was a uniform blanket of cloud, and a persistent, icy sleet fell, stinging her face with every gust of wind.

Despite Agnes's words of reassurance, she felt uneasy. There was no grand plan, only a grim determination to attend this masque. The murderer would strike again, she was certain of it. Meanwhile, Mr Pepys languished in a jail cell, an innocent pawn in very dark game.

Something had to give. She just needed a stroke of good fortune.

Abby had lost hope of seeing Jacob again. *As he abandoned me, so I abandon him*, she thought. The words felt hollow.

She had viewed the Great Hall before, since it lay just behind the Great Chapel, where Sophie de Valois's body had been taken. The grand Tudor relic was said to have been built by Cardinal Wolsey, who was also responsible for Hampton Court Palace - clearly a gentleman with grandeur on his mind.

Abby knew her history: Wolsey fell out with Henry VIII having failed to secure an annulment of his marriage to Catherine of Aragon, and died of dysentery on his way to face trial for treason. A bitter end for a man of such ambitious taste, as was so often the way.

What will be Hakewill's fate today? she wondered.

Bells declaring the eleventh hour had lately rung as the maids approached the towering stone edifice. Servants laden with ornate decor jostled for space with performers in colourful, often outlandish costumes, as they made their way to the grand entrance. The stained-glass windows with their heraldic designs towered above Abby, and her eyes were drawn to the intricately carved oriel window jutting from the upper wall.

Nervously, she glanced about, searching for familiar faces, and was relieved to see none. Naturally, however, as the King's erstwhile guest, it was mostly the wealthy courtiers she had encountered - and they were yet to arrive.

"Quickly!" barked Agnes from the head of the line, pausing to let the maids file past her into the hall.

Once inside, Abby was struck by the sheer scale and majesty of the space. She could not help but gawp, her eyes drawn to heraldic banners hanging from the high roof beams and the flood of coloured light streaming in through the stained-glass windows. As she lingered, awestruck, the maid behind her collided into her back, drawing sniggers from a pair of passing musicians.

Agnes appeared at her side in an instant. "Do not make a spectacle of yourself," she scolded.

Abby could only bow her head.

She was on edge - a dangerous place to be. *Be calm,* she urged herself. Particularly fearful for Molly Tanner's safety, she needed to locate the young actor's seat. If the murderer planned to strike again, she was convinced that Molly would be their target. After all, she had received that ominous note.

Abby took in the wondrous scene that stretched before her.

Temporary galleries lined either side of the hall, filled with seating. In the centre, supported by a wooden frame, the rear of a vast canvas backdrop obscured her view of the far end.

Only when she had followed the line of maids down the right side of the hall did the full magnificence of the layout become apparent. In front of the backdrop was a raised stage, its sides draped in rich fabrics. At the far end of the hall, where she now stood, was a raised dais, bearing a pair of gilded thrones beneath a crimson canopy of state. From such a vantage point, King Charles and Queen Catherine – seated side by side for once – could command the finest views of the afternoon's entertainment.

Rows of seating stretched from the dais toward the stage, arranged in orderly tiers reflecting courtly rank. Closest to the stage were the finest chairs, intricately carved; behind them sat simpler wooden benches for courtiers of lesser status.

A constant hum of activity echoed about the space. Musicians tuned instruments, jugglers juggled, acrobats practised tumbles, dancers fussed over costumes, and actors emoted in preparation for their moment under the kingly gaze.

Abby, meanwhile, found herself in a huddle of maids gathered on the dais, awaiting instruction. "Polish Her Majesty's throne," Agnes told Abby, handing her a cloth and a pot of oil.

She was still polishing – it was an extravagant throne – when the general thrum of the Great Hall suddenly changed pitch. Trumpeters in regal tabards were taking their stations, sending panicked performers scrambling for their seats in the galleries.

Agnes tapped Abby on the shoulder and beckoned her to join the other Maids of Honour, who were now arranged in rows at the rear of the dais.

The time had flown by. Abby had intended to track down Molly's seat, but the opportunity had slipped away. *If the murderer is to act again,* she wondered, *what abhorrent sabotage might they concoct here?*

Her eyes drifted upward to the vast, multi-tiered chandeliers suspended from great rafters in the ceiling. With their scrolled brass arms and countless beeswax candles, they were as impressive as they were ominous. *Might Molly have been strategically placed beneath one?* Abby wondered, reasoning that a single fall would cause serious harm or death to anyone in the vicinity.

She dismissed the idea. The murderer would not use the same method twice. Whoever they were, they were too clever for that.

Then how?

A fanfare of trumpets echoed throughout the hall, bringing the masque in honour of Henry Wyndham to life.

Chapter Thirty-Eight

The Masque

Those gathered in the Great Hall fell silent as the fanfare faded, and a group of musicians in one of the galleries struck up a stately tune on violins, lutes, and sackbuts. Leading them was a guitar virtuoso, announced as Francesco Corbetta.

The main doors opened, and Abby caught sight of the King and Queen entering, flanked by attendants bearing the symbols of royal authority: orb, sceptre, and tall, slender banners mounted on poles. In their wake, she saw Arabella Wyndham, mere yards from her rival the Queen, trailed by her son clad in full regalia. Behind them came a seemingly endless procession of the great and good of the King's court, a dazzling display of colour and pageantry that lifted even Abby's shaken spirits.

As she peered about for Molly Tanner, like a punch to the gut, the realisation struck her: she was seated in the front row of the Maids of Honour - directly in Charles's line of sight. How could she have been so careless? Anxiously, she glanced around. *Dare I move back and risk drawing attention to myself?* she wondered.

Behind her, Agnes caught her eye and glared. *Hold your nerve*, the look said.

Bowing her head low, striving to appear reverential rather than suspicious, she observed the approaching procession from beneath her brow. Her heart pounded.

As the King mounted the short flight of steps to the dais, his gaze appeared fixed on her, and Abby wished the wooden platform would swallow her whole. Was he now walking directly towards her? *Is that anger in his face?* she wondered, clenching her jaw.

Thoughts swirling, the inquisitor was barely resisting the urge to flee when Charles abruptly turned left and took a seat on his throne.

It was Queen Catherine of Braganza who now advanced on her, wearing an expression of perplexed curiosity.

"Quem é você?"

Her Majesty was addressing Abby - in Portuguese. The Queen's dark eyes studied her beneath thick black brows. She wore a black velvet gown, a jewelled crucifix glinting at her throat.

"Quem é você?" Catherine repeated, her tone sharper now.

Please don't draw attention to me, Abby thought, blurting out the one phrase Agnes had taught her. "Eu não entendo."

The Queen's expression shifted to bewilderment.

Charles swivelled on his throne, peering back at them. "My love…?" he called, his gaze flicking from Catherine to Abby.

Self-consciously, Abby scratched her forehead, partially concealing her face. When she lowered her hand, Charles had already turned back, and she exhaled in relief.

Catherine seized Abby's arm, shaking it forcefully. "Quem é você?" she demanded, her voice rising.

Abby could only shake her head, her lips trapped in a rictus grin. Just then, Agnes stepped forward. "Her Majesty wishes to know who you are," she whispered in Abby's ear.

Agnes bowed to Catherine and began speaking in fluent Portuguese. The Queen's severe expression gradually softened. When they finished, Catherine turned to Abby.

"Agnes tells me you are new," she said in a thick accent, offering a brief smile. "Welcome, Eleanor."

And with that, she swept away.

"I told her your name was Eleanor," Agnes murmured, retaking her place.

With everyone settled into their places, the entertainment began.

On the stage, a pair of rope dancers thrilled the audience with daring feats on a thick rope stretched across the platform. The first, the celebrated funambulist Jacob Hall, attired in purple and white silks, balanced with effortless grace, wielding a long pole for steadiness. His female partner, dressed in a vivid green tunic, sprang lightly onto the rope, drawing audible gasps. She spun deftly in place, arms outstretched, before somersaulting backward in a dazzling display of skill.

Both dancers wore shimmering golden papier-mâché masks, fashioned in the image of a mythological sun god, secured by red silk ribbons trailing from the backs of their heads.

Beneath them, a drummer seated at the foot of the stage tapped out a rhythmic beat, heightening the drama of the performance. Abby's eyes flicked briefly to the painted backdrop - a grand manor house surrounded by lush woodlands. It was the estate Henry Wyndham and his mother schemed to claim, she imagined.

Yet Abby's mind was not on the Wyndhams' connivances, nor on the daring display holding the audience spellbound. Her gaze flitted over the backs of the spectators' heads, searching for a sign of Molly Tanner. A sickly sense of dread tightened her chest.

Arabella and Henry, seated as guests of honour, commanded the central seats in the front row. Beside Arabella, Abby noted the powdered grey periwig and imposing bulk of Sir William Hakewill, who appeared more intent upon the entertainment than murder.

On either side of those three figures stretched a blur of periwigs and hats - powdered, curled, and jauntily feathered – blending into a sea of finery. Abby soon found it impossible to tell where one delightfully adorned head ended and another began, all merging into an indistinct mass of sartorial extravagance.

She scanned desperately for the loose auburn curls and petite figure of Molly Tanner; no such figure emerged among the crowd.

Then she saw it.

A gap in the seating, three or four chairs in front of Hakewill.

A gap.

What if she's not here? Abby thought. *And if she isn't here - then where is she?*

Chapter Thirty-Nine

An Unexpected Entrance

A troupe of masked performers took the stage, dressed as figures from classical mythology. Mars, god of war, in a crimson robe, wielding a sword. Opposite him, Venus, goddess of love, draped in white with a garland of flowers in her hair, hands clasped in a gesture of pleading. Between them, Discord, cloaked in black, dagger poised to strike at the very heart of Mars.

The musical accompaniment, tense and discordant, came to an abrupt halt as the tableau onstage froze, and the audience held its collective breath.

There came the sounds of commotion from the rear of the hall. The performers, professional to a man, remained stock still, frozen in their staged fight, but murmurs began to ripple through the spectators.

Abby craned her neck and gasped as a servant emerged from behind the backdrop. Draped in his arms was the lifeless figure of a young woman, dressed only in her shift.

The young woman was Molly Tanner.

The King shot bolt upright, crying out, "Molly! My love!"

From where Abby stood, she could not see the Queen's expression.

Charles descended the royal platform and rushed to meet the servant, as a wave of shock and indignation swept through the crowd. Guards rushed forward, but the King angrily waved them aside.

"I… I found her in her bed, Sire," the servant stammered. "She was… dead."

Taking Molly's body gently from him, the King sank to his knees, cradling his mistress in his arms. "Why?" he beseeched the heavens.

Those gathered watched, some outraged, others struck with compassion. A few wept openly for the King, while others leaned close to their neighbours, furtively muttering.

"How…?" the King asked pitifully, his voice breaking. "Her eyes…"

"Aye, Sire," the servant replied, shifting uneasily. "They… They're red with blood."

Charles's eyes blazed. "Was she murdered?"

The servant, out of his depth, seemed ready to flee. "Sire, 'tis not for me to say." Under the King's glare, he added hastily, "But her skin, Sire. 'Tis darkened about her neck and torso."

The King rose with a low, animal growl. His fur-trimmed cloak flailed behind him as he strode from the hall, cradling his young mistress. His footsteps echoed like Death's rap on the door of a plague house.

When Hakewill rose to follow, Abby acted on instinct.

Running, she leapt from the dais, drawing grasps from onlookers, and gave chase.

Outside, she found the King still clutching Molly's lifeless form, in urgent discourse with his adviser. Catching her breath, she joined them, casting off her coif and letting her long hair fall to her shoulders.

The King's face flushed crimson. "You!" he snarled. "I ordered you to leave my palace!"

Hakewill regarded her with calm detachment.

Abby wrapped her arms around herself. "Sire, I beg you…"

The King thrust Molly's body into Hakewill's arms, grabbed Abby's gown and hauled her close, forcing her onto her tiptoes. "What is the meaning of this subterfuge? What game do you play?" he demanded.

"I know who murdered your mistresses," Abby replied, studiously avoiding Hakewill's gaze.

The King's grip slackened, and he let his hand fall. His long cheeks paled, and he asked, almost in a whisper, "What say you?"

"I believe I know who…"

He cut her off abruptly. "Come!" he barked, turning on his heel.

As Charles stormed off towards his apartments, Hakewill cast Abby a scornful smile before following in the King's wake. Grimacing, the young inquisitor hurried after them.

None of them had noticed the tall figure crouched behind one of the Great Hall's buttresses, eavesdropping. As Abby disappeared around a corner, he rose and bolted after her, adjusting his tatty periwig as he went.

Chapter Forty

The Unmasking

Abby found herself in the King's private chamber, a space so opulent it seemed almost otherworldly. Portraits of mistresses, some depicted in little but seductive expressions, adorned the walls, while the air carried the scent of exotic spices. A gilded bed with heavy, embroidered drapes dominated the room, and every surface gleamed with gold, silver or polished wood, reflecting the flicker of so many candles.

The room had no windows. It was designed for discretion.

The body of Molly Tanner lay sprawled across the velvet blankets. Only now did Abby notice the ring on her finger: the Standish family ring.

Shaking her head in sorrow, she turned away.

The King stood before her, Hakewill at his side.

It struck Abby that she had no idea how Molly had died, and that her evidence against the King's adviser was flimsy at best. But she had made her move - boldly, as Mr

Pepys would have wished – and she had no choice now but to press on.

Her employer's life was at stake.

"Well?" the King snapped, anger burning his features. "Tell me who murdered my loves."

Abby took a deep breath. "Sire, I believe it was…"

The chamber door flew open, and a young man stumbled inside, sprawling onto all fours at the King's feet. Startled, His Majesty recoiled as Hakewill bellowed, "Where are the guards?"

The interloper raised his gaze to the King, pushed himself to his feet, and announced, "Sire, I fear my sister murdered your mistresses – and I can prove it."

"Standish?" the King exclaimed.

"Jacob!" Abby gasped, stepping forward, her delight turning to shock as she froze mid-step. "Hold… What say you?" she stammered. "Your sister? Anne?" Her voice trembled with dismay. "But Jacob, she's dead."

Before he could respond, a pair of guards burst into the room.

"Seize him!" Hakewill barked.

The King raised a hand. "Hold! I will hear his words."

Abby stared at His Majesty, baffled. *He, of all men, knows she is dead.*

"Leave us," the King commanded the guards. "And let no man enter."

What in God's name is happening? Abby wondered, running a trembling hand through her hair.

As he spoke, Jacob rummaged through his satchel. "I gained entry to Anne's apartment," he said, "and discovered…"

"But her door was locked. I tried it," Abby interjected, struggling to make sense of his words.

Jacob held up a ring of pointed lock-picking tools. "Quigley," he said simply, before continuing. "I found this among the papers in her chamber – the same chamber from which all are barred. Even…" His glance flicked to the King, who cleared his throat awkwardly.

Abby took the small, triangular scrap of paper Jacob handed her. The words scribbled on it seemed nonsensical:

Miles
is note with
cretion to the
n who must
ht in the

Then it dawned on her. "The missing piece of the note we discovered on Sophie de Valois's body," she said.

"Aye," Jacob replied. "You have it?"

In a daze, Abby nodded and produced her copied note from a leather pocket hung about her neck.

> *Sir*
> *Deliver th*
> *the utmost dis*
> *lady I did mentio*
> *await me at midnig*
> *Vane Room.*
> *Trust none but her.*
> *Yours in confidence*
> *Samuel Pepys*

"So 'twas addressed to Sir Miles, your father, all along," Abby said, her tone laced with disbelief.

"As children, I told you, when we disobeyed Father, we were sent on errands, delivering such notes for him. Anne was ever the most disobedient. 'Tis now apparent that she never delivered them but kept them in secret. That one, she used to frame…" Jacob faltered, his voice cracking. "To frame the goodly Mr Pepys."

Abby struggled to make sense of it all. "Molly Tanner also received a note," she said. "'Mary lies in shallow waters. We must tread carefully, or she will flounder.' The name Mary had been altered to read 'Molly.' It meant little to us at the time."

Jacob sighed. "Another of my sister's collection, I fear. As apprentice purser, I am acquainted with a royal yacht named Mary." He glanced at the King, who gave a curt nod of affirmation.

"Oh, Jacob," Abby gasped, barely above a whisper. "Can it be true? That her death was…" She trailed off, her gaze shifting to Charles.

The King imperiously raised his chin as all eyes turned to him.

"Continue, Standish," he snapped.

"But Sire…"

"I said continue!"

Abby turned to Jacob, her voice trembling with emotion. "How did you know?"

"Quigley helped me see the truth. It was always there, but I was too blinded by loyalty to Anne to admit it." He placed a hand on Abby's shoulder, gaze downcast. "Instead, I directed my anger and frustration toward you, dearest Abby." Dropping to his knees, he implored her, "Can you ever forgive me?"

"A most touching display," the King interrupted dryly, "but I am more eager to hear of your deductions, Standish. What is this truth of which you speak?"

Jacob straightened, gathering himself. He recounted how, as children, his sisters would hide small items in the hems of their dresses - just as the note had been concealed on Mistress de Valois. He spoke of Anne's penchant for mischief and games: the broken chair she had once offered him, a memory that now so chillingly mirrored the sabotage that had claimed the lives of the King's mistresses.

"Quigley urged me to return here and inspect Anne's residence," Jacob continued. "He said if she were innocent, my search could do no harm. 'Tis when I found the missing piece of the note," his head dropped, "which proved her guilt."

The room was ominously silent as Jacob reached into his satchel and extracted a strange object. "I found this as well, hidden in a chest in Anne's chamber." He held up a long, translucent sheath, coiled and eerily patterned. "I know not what..."

Hakewill stepped forward, taking the object delicately between thumb and forefinger. "The shed skin of a snake," he said. "It seems Mistress Standish kept one."

Abby's eyes widened. "The French ambassador gifted His Majesty a python," she said. "It later vanished."

Jacob nodded grimly. "It would explain the rodents in her chamber - sustenance for the creature. She did always hanker after her own menagerie." Suddenly, he started. "Her parrot warned of a snake! Anne told me the snake was me!"

"That sound I heard," Abby added softly, almost to herself. "'Twas not Sir William's breathing. 'Twas the python."

Hakewill raised an eyebrow, his words laced with irony. "Mistress Harcourt, how gracious of you to imagine me skulking among serpents."

Jacob moved toward the bed where Molly lay, her bloodshot eyes staring blankly. "Your Majesty, I overheard your discourse with the servant who discovered Molly's body," he said. "I was hiding among the musicians in a nearby gallery." He hesitated, then added, "They handed me a sackbut to play, but I could not."

"What is your point, Standish?" Charles demanded.

"Sire, I wonder… Did the same snake squeeze the life from this poor lady? It would explain the marks on her body."

The King's fury erupted. "She has overstepped all bounds! Anne! Anne!" he bellowed, his face crimson with rage. "Show yourself!"

A door behind him creaked open, and into the room stepped Anne Standish.

Chapter Forty-One

A Stark Choice

The King ranted and raged, shaking Anne Standish so violently that Hakewill, visibly reluctant, was forced to intervene. Only after much persuasion did Charles begin to calm.

Anne, for her part, remained blank-faced, while Abby and Jacob looked on helplessly.

Shortly, Abby stepped forward. "Sire, may I speak freely?"

"Indeed you may, Abigail," Charles replied with an unsettling smile. "Since your words will never reach another's ears but ours."

"You faked Anne's death," she told His Majesty bluntly.

He nodded. "We had an arrangement, Anne and I." Resolutely, he avoided meeting his mistress's gaze. "After she lay with Loxley - to my great sorrow, being so new to my own bed - I threatened to have her executed." A faint smile flickered on his lips. "To save her hide, she offered me a bargain. She claimed she would… remove Sophie from my court. I had secretly harboured a notion to achieve the same, through politicking and subterfuge. I assumed she meant to make poor Sophie's life so unbearable that she would long to return to France. Instead, as is her wont, Anne overstepped and took the lady's life."

"When I first learned of it, I was incandescent with rage. But then," he shook his head, drolly amused, "her death began to seem convenient. Sophie's espionage had nearly drawn us into war with France, yet I dared not act against her myself. She was a liability - and I had grown weary of her. And now, as far as everybody was concerned, she was gone, apparently at the hand of some foul miscreant. As only I realised, the miscreant was Anne."

The full weight of the King's callousness settled over the room.

"And to protect her," Abby said, "you removed the nails from Anne's door yourself, to stage her demise?"

"I did," he replied, looking rather pleased with himself. "It fooled you all."

"If I may, Sire?" Jacob interjected meekly. "While your guards assaulted me, I managed to drag Anne's arm free. It occurred to me only later, given the weight of the door, that such a feat should not have been possible. The door must have been propped up."

Abby's eyes widened. "The broken tiles I saw outside Anne's house the following morning!" she cried, then paused as another realisation struck. "And your family ring, Jacob… She stole it, all along, using it for her murderous games."

"He never deserved it." The words, stated coldly, came from Anne Standish's mouth. At last, the defiant young mistress had found her voice.

Jacob turned to his sister, expression pleading. "What mean you, Anne?"

"I mean you never deserved that ring, Jacob. Your worth is but a fraction of our dead brothers'." Gliding to the King's side, she slipped her arm through his. "Charlie…"

Enraged, he bore down on her. "I am not your Charlie!" he thundered. "I am your King!"

Yet Anne stood her ground. "Sire, you wished Sophie gone. I did you a favour."

"Then you took it too far, you wicked wench!" he railed. "You murdered my precious Molly as well!"

Anne shrugged. "You need no other mistress but me."

Charles seemed fit to explode. "I shall be the judge of that! I, Charles, King of England, Scotland, and Ireland!"

Hakewill had heard enough. "Then her fate is sealed," he said.

The King turned to him, lips sombrely set. "I fear 'tis not that simple, Sir William."

Charles pointed out that the five people in that room - and those five alone - knew of his subterfuge. Prior to Molly's demise, he had intended to return Anne to his court once the inquisitors had departed, as if nothing had happened. "And none within these palace walls would suspect her murderous act against my Sophie," the King concluded.

"I would have heard tell of it," Jacob muttered, avoiding His Majesty's eye. "She is my sister."

"And you would spread word of it?" the King asked, his tone laced with menace.

Jacob, downcast, shook his head, all too aware of the consequences.

Charles turned to Abigail. "And you, my dear? Would you... tell all?"

"Indeed not, Sire," she replied quietly.

The collective gaze drifted to Hakewill.

The King laughed. "My good friend, Sir William's lips are sealed, I am sure." When Hakewill remained silent, he added, "Since I am certain he would not wish it known that he pilfers valuables from the dead. Hmm?"

Hakewill studiously inspected his fingernails.

"Then the matter is closed, Sire?" Jacob ventured cautiously.

"I fear not, Standish," the King replied. His gaze shifted toward Anne. "Now that my dear mistress has so recklessly murdered Mistress Tanner - in full view of most every noble in the country – somebody must be seen to pay. The people will scent blood."

"And Anne is guilty of the crime," Abby pointed out, glaring at Jacob's sister.

Anne snorted, as a thin smile played on the King's lips. "You forget, my dear," he told Abby, "that your Mr Pepys is already accused of Sophie's murder."

Abby's chin fell.

Jacob, horrified, stammered, "B–but Sire, he remains incarcerated and could not possibly have murdered Mistress Tanner."

The King pressed his fingertips together. "Or did I release him ere the terrible event occurred, that he was free to strike again?"

"You cannot…!" Abby gasped.

"Oh, but I can," Charles interrupted, as Hakewill looked on impassively.

Jacob dropped to his knees, wringing his hands before the King. "Sire, Your Majesty, I beg you, do not condemn an innocent man. Mr Pepys is…"

The King raised a hand for silence, eyes cold. "I offer you a choice, Jacob Standish. Your sister – or your beloved Pepys?"

"Nay, Sire!" Jacob croaked, his voice breaking, as Abby threw herself at the King's feet. "Your Majesty, please…" she implored.

He toed her aside without a glance.

Chapter Forty-Two

Departure

The mood was sombre as the inquisitors made their way down the Privy Stairs toward their waiting wherry. Behind them came a sudden cry. "Jacob! Abigail!"

Turning, they saw Samuel Pepys hobbling toward them. His gait was unsteady from his recent ordeal, but his face was alight with joy at his newfound freedom.

Abby and Jacob stopped to allow him to catch up, and the three embraced as if they would never let go. "How can I thank you enough?" Pepys said, his voice thick with emotion.

The inquisitors, too, were overcome. It had been a harrowing end to a grim investigation, and they longed only to return to their homes, far removed from the King's court and its abhorrent corruption.

There was, at least, one small reprieve. After much pleading from Jacob on behalf of his sister, the King had decreed that Anne's punishment would be banishment from the kingdom. Anne's blood was not on Jacob's hands, which he knew he could not have borne.

In truth, he could not bear to set eyes on her again.

As the three friends boarded the wherry, they were startled by another voice calling out, accompanied by hurried footsteps on the wooden decking.

"Hold!" the voice cried. "Hold!"

To Abby's astonishment, it belonged to Arabella Wyndham.

Arabella stopped at the top of the steps leading down to the river, peering into the boat.

Always looking down on me, Abby thought to herself.

"Abigail," Arabella said, clasping her hands together in an uncharacteristic display of gratitude. "I must thank you for all you have done these past days. Poor Molly is dead," she added. "And it seems you saved my life."

Abby blinked, stunned. "I… I… You should thank my fellow inquisitor, Jacob, Arabella, for 'twas he who…"

Jacob nudged her sharply in the ribs and called up to the mistress on the pier. "Do you recall asking Abigail," he adopted Arabella's mocking tone, "what is it you do *inquisit?*"

Arabella shook her head, puzzled. But Abby remembered. She remembered it well, and hid a mischievous grin.

"Well, now you know," Jacob told her, adding with a dismissive wave of his hand, "Would you kindly be gone?"

The day was bitterly cold and grey, yet the mood in the wherry grew lighter with every creak of the oars, as Pepys and his inquisitors put more distance between themselves and Whitehall Palace.

"What next, I wonder, Mr Pepys?" Jacob asked.

"I believe we all need a good rest, Mr Standish," Pepys replied with a sigh. "And after that? Who knows what the future holds?" He drew his coat tightly around himself and glanced skyward. "'Tis fearful cold. Perhaps snow will come and cloak this burned city in a mantle of white."

Noticing Abby shivering, Jacob removed the hat from his head and placed it on hers. "I would like that very much," she said, smiling up at her friend.

If you enjoyed this book, please consider leaving a rating or review – they are greatly appreciated and genuinely help.

Next up: it's Christmas, the Thames freezes over and all London takes to the ice, in The Samuel Pepys Mysteries Book 5: The Frost Fair Murders.

Amazon link: mybook.to/pepys-series

- "This series just gets better with every book" – *Rambling Mads*

- "A must if you love a historical cozy mystery" – *LJ Writes & Reviews*

- "Abby is my absolute favourite – her portrayal as a headstrong woman in this period makes me smile." – *My Book Journey*

Read All Nine!

mybook.to/pepys-series

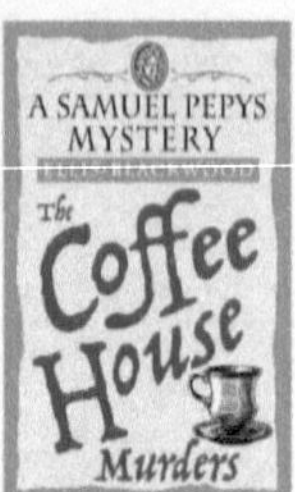

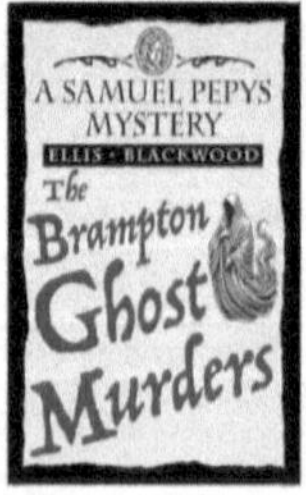

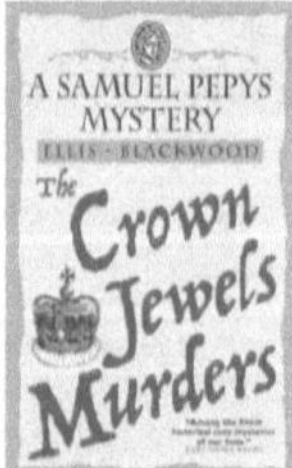

Ellis Blackwood

Ellis Blackwood fell in love with the writings of Samuel Pepys and the 17th-century England he so colourfully portrays via the great man's published diaries. The Samuel Pepys Mysteries are the result of that literary love affair.

Ellis lives on the coast of Cornwall with his wife, two daughters and dog, Spike. A former journalist, he wrote features for many of the UK's most popular national newspapers and magazines. During the COVID lockdown, he gained an MA in Comedy Writing.

Visit my website ellisblackwood.com for all release updates, and to subscribe to my monthly newsletter – including the FREE Pepys Mysteries introductory novella, Mr Pepys's Stolen Diaries.

Find me on Facebook @ellisblackwoodauthor

And on Instagram @ellisblackwood_author

Scan the QR code for all my links.

Acknowledgements

I could not have published The Samuel Pepys Myster-ies without the sterling work of Tim Brown, whose covers are a joy to behold, and whose editorial guidance has been a godsend. Equally, my wife, Sinead, has worked tirelessly and generously in the background to allow me the time and space to research, write, and drink far too much tea.

If you'd like to learn more about Samuel Pepys and 17th century England, I recommend starting here:

- *The Illustrated Pepys* edited by Robert Latham, Penguin Books (1979)

- *London and the 17th Century* by Margarette Lincoln, Yale University Press (2021)

- *Samuel Pepys: The Unequalled Self* by Claire

Tomalin, Penguin Books (2003)

- *The Time Traveller's Guide to Restoration Britain* by Ian Mortimer, The Bodley Head (2017)

In my monthly newsletters, I deep-dive into the fascinating historical background to each novel, from the Princes in the Tower to the ingredients of posset. Visit ellisblackwood.comto sign up.